Library of Congress-in-Publication Data
A Ring of Deception / by DeAnna Julie Dodson
p. cm.
I. Title
                    2016945690

CountrySamplerFiction.com
(800) 282-6643
Antique Shop Mysteries™
Series Creator: Shari Lohner
Series Editor: Shari Lohner
Cover Illustrator: Bonnie Leick

10 11 12 13 14 | Printed in China | 9 8 7 6 5 4 3 2 1

"The average man will bristle if you say his father was dishonest, but he will brag a little if he discovers that his great-grandfather was a pirate."

—Bernard Williams

1

Maggie Watson tried to hide a smile as she watched June McGillis, her friend who managed Carriage House Antiques. June had her purse slung over one shoulder and her car keys in her hand as she poked around the cash register. Maggie eyed the precariously balanced manila folder full of papers wedged in the crook of her arm.

Though she already knew the answer, Maggie asked, "What'd you lose?"

"Nothing." June ran a hand through her short, strawberry-blond hair in frustration.

Maggie chuckled. "Try that little marble-topped end table over by the window."

June scurried over to the table and scooped up the cloisonné ballpoint pen she wore on a chain around her neck. "Your aunt was so wise to give this to me. Now if I could only remember to wear it." Grinning widely, she slipped it over her head. "All right. I'm off to the bank. I'll be back in a jiffy."

"I'll hold down the fort."

June hurried out, and Maggie sighed contentedly. It had been several months since Aunt Evelyn had died and left her the shop, and she felt more at home in Somerset Harbor with each passing day. She thanked God and Aunt Evelyn for bringing her to the quaint town. She was doing something she loved, surrounded by good people who cared about her. Not everyone was able to realize such a dream. She even had patient, savvy June to help her learn the antiques business. In addition to all that, it was a pretty day trying valiantly to turn into spring.

June had mentioned wanting to do a display with the pair of carved Louis XVI-style walnut fauteuils they'd recently acquired. The chairs were upholstered in powder blue, and Maggie wanted to add a few coordinating items that would emphasize the color. June would probably end up changing some of her vignette, but Maggie was determined to give it a try anyway.

She found a blue-and-gold vase with baroque accents and a wide bolt of shot silk, also powder blue but with a shimmer of gold when the light hit it the right way. June could most likely turn it into a tablecloth or some kind of drape behind the chairs. As she was adding a porcelain clock to the collection, the bell over the door jingled.

Maggie looked up. "Hello."

The girl at the door was dressed in jeans and a dark-gray hoodie with a coral-and-teal T-shirt peeking out at the collar. She didn't have a purse, but there was the visible outline of a cell phone in her pocket.

"Uh, hi," the girl replied.

She was young, maybe seventeen. Maybe not even that. Partially hidden by the dishwater-blond hair that fell over her heart-shaped face, her dark eyes were earnest and a bit wary.

Maggie smiled warmly, trying to make her feel more at ease. "Can I help you?"

The girl blinked. "I . . . was wondering if you buy old stuff. Antiques, I mean."

"We do. Do you have something you'd like to sell?"

"Yes. It's just a ring, but it's gold."

Maggie was about to suggest she take it to the local jeweler, but then the girl fished in her pocket and brought it out.

"Oh my." That was all Maggie could say as the girl set it on the counter.

"It's gold," the girl repeated, casting an anxious glance at the door. "And that's a real emerald."

Maggie nodded absently, too fascinated by the ring to really listen. It was old and lavishly ornate—a man's ring, judging by the size and heaviness of it. A man of some consequence, she didn't doubt. *And a man of the sea, apparently.*

The emerald was large and of good quality, and the head and upper body of a golden sea serpent slithered over it with the rest of its scaly body and long tail wrapped around the gem. Circling the snake's body was a ship's wheel marked with the four points of the compass. And along the band, with crossed cutlasses at its head and feet, was a bas-relief skeleton. It was somehow beautiful, morbid, and gaudy all at once.

"This looks like a pirate's ring," Maggie said. "It's fascinating. Where did you get it?"

The girl shrugged. "It's been in the family a long time. I don't know anything about it except that it's real gold, and the emerald is real."

"You don't know how old it is?"

"Older than me," the girl said. "How much will you give me for it?"

"Well, I'm not sure yet. I'll have to do some checking and make sure—"

"I'm sorry." The girl quickly swept the ring back into her pocket. "I really can't wait. But thanks for talking to me." She turned toward the door.

"Wait."

The girl peeked back over her shoulder, and Maggie felt her heart twinge. The wariness in the girl's eyes was even more pronounced than before. Maggie couldn't help but think of Emily all on her own now. What if there was something wrong, and this girl had nowhere to turn?

"Are you in trouble?" Maggie asked gently.

"No. What makes you think that?" The girl's soft mouth turned down, and she lifted her chin. "I need some money, and I thought this would be a good place to sell my ring. There are other places."

"Let me see the ring again."

Maggie held out her hand, and after a moment's uncertainty, the girl put the ring in it. It felt heavy enough to be real gold. Maggie rummaged in a drawer and brought out the jeweler's loupe. Telltale imperfections indicated that the stone wasn't man-made. Then she took out the piece of unglazed ceramic June sometimes used to test whether a piece of jewelry was genuine gold. She rubbed the band of the ring against the ceramic, and it left a gold mark. If it had been gold-plated, the mark would have been black. Everything seemed on the up-and-up. She wished June were here now to advise her, but Maggie didn't want the girl to go somewhere she might be taken advantage of.

"I'll be honest with you," Maggie said finally. "I think this ring is worth more than I have lying around here in cash."

"How much could you—"

"If you need some money, why don't you let me give you, say, $500?"

The girl's dark eyes widened. "Five hundred?"

"As a down payment so you'll have some money until I can find out what it's really worth. Then you can come back and I'll make you a reasonable offer. How would that be?"

The girl's eyes narrowed. "Umm, yeah. Okay."

"Don't worry, I'll give you a receipt for it. What's your name?"

"Uh." The girl licked her lips. "Uh, Gail Lee. L-E-E."

"Okay. This will take just a minute or two. Regulations, you know."

Maggie snapped a couple of pictures of the ring for the sales records and then filled out the appropriate form, including the weight and description of the ring, and noted that the $500 she would be giving the girl was only a partial payment until they got a proper appraisal.

"I'll need to see your driver's license too," Maggie said, wondering if the girl even had one yet.

Gail fumbled in her pocket and pulled out a license with her photo on it. It listed her name and an address in a little town a few miles down the coast. Maggie added the information in the appropriate blanks on the sales form and then gave her a statement of ownership to sign. The girl didn't seem to hesitate over the bolded sentence at the bottom, warning that making a false statement was a Class D misdemeanor. She signed *Gail Lee*, the letters a little awkward, but legible.

After that, Maggie had Gail sign a receipt for the money. Then she got $500 out of the brass cash register. If this turned out to be a scam, she would never hear the end of it from June. *But surely a ring like this is worth at least $500?* She felt certain there was a fascinating story behind it.

"All right," Maggie said when she had paid the girl. "You can call or come see me in a couple of days, and I'll let you know what I've found out. Deal?" She handed Gail one of the shop's business cards.

"Deal."

The girl stuffed the card and money into the front pocket of her hoodie and headed for the door.

"Wait a minute."

Gail froze and then slowly peered over her shoulder.

Maggie smiled and held up the receipt for the ring. "Aren't you forgetting something?"

"Oh." The girl took the receipt and then scampered out the door.

Maggie picked up the ring, examining it again. "What is June going to say? But aren't you the most fascinating thing? Whoever commissioned this must have been quite a character."

It would take someone larger than life to wear something so bold. The sea serpent and the ship's wheel were definite ties to sailing. The cutlasses and the skeleton seemed more of a warning, a notice that the bearer was not to be trifled with. Maggie would have to find out more. There had been pirates up and down the coast in the early part of the eighteenth century. Maybe this had belonged to one of them.

The bell on the door jingled again, and Maggie looked up to see June breeze in.

"Did I miss anything?"

Maggie grinned sheepishly. "You're going to kill me."

. . . .

"Gail Lee?" June gaped at the signature scrawled on the receipt and then at the ring.

"I filled out all the appropriate paperwork and saw her driver's license," Maggie said, still anxious about the situation.

"I don't know of any Lees in the area, but I guess there might be some over in Merritt or down in Selden. I'll have to ask Ruth if she's heard of any. But really, Maggie, $500?"

"You said it was worth much more than that," Maggie protested.

"If it was hers to sell in the first place. Where would a girl like that get this kind of thing if she hadn't stolen it?"

Maggie sighed. Of course she had wondered the same thing herself, but she hadn't been able to simply turn the girl away. "Gail said it had been in her family for a long time. Maybe a grandfather or great-uncle passed it down to her. Or maybe it came from a very generous aunt." She grinned. "Those things *do* happen."

"You softie," June said. "At least you got her license number, though I doubt it's any good. We'll find out what this thing is really worth. And then, when the girl doesn't call or come back, I'll say I told you so."

"Why wouldn't she return? If she wants money and the ring is worth more than I gave her for it, she'd want to get the rest."

June put her hands on her hips. "Not if she stole it in the first place. She'd want to get whatever she could for it and clear out. She could be headed to Boise right now."

Maggie glanced toward the door, seeing again the slim figure with the drab hoodie and the frightened dark eyes in her mind. "I wish I'd found out more about what was going on with her, but she didn't give me much chance to talk. She was going to take the ring somewhere else if I didn't give her something for it. I don't think she has a clue what it's worth, so I didn't want some other place taking advantage of her. She definitely didn't know its provenance. I couldn't let her leave with nothing. Besides," she said, picking up the ring, "this is an amazing piece. I think even Cap'n Jack Sparrow would be tempted by it."

June finally cracked a smile. "You just hope Johnny Depp will show up in his pirate movie costume and claim it."

Maggie didn't protest.

"That ring's very unusual, I'll give you that. I'd love to know who'd be flamboyant enough to wear such a thing." June leaned closer to the ring, squinting slightly. "I'd also like to know what the inscription means."

"Inscription?" Maggie regarded it more closely. "How'd I miss that?"

"It's nearly worn off, but it's there on the inside of the band."

Maggie rummaged in one of the drawers behind the counter and found the magnifying glass. "Write this down." She attempted to pronounce the words, then gave up and spelled them: *Conrigi vix tandem quod curvom est factum crede.*

June used her pen to jot it down. Then her forehead wrinkled. "Any idea what it means?"

"Not a clue," Maggie said. "But I'm going to find out."

"Mom, I want to come home."

The pleasure Maggie had felt when she first answered the phone that evening turned to sympathy and concern. She sat down on the couch and immediately got a lap full of chubby tabby. Her cat, Snickers, had apparently been waiting for this opportunity.

"What's wrong, honey?"

There was only a choked silence on the other end of the line.

"Emily?" Maggie urged.

Her daughter partly sobbed as she took a breath. "It's all too hard. I've got so much homework and then clinicals, and I'm so tired. And my preceptor has been sick all week."

Maggie frowned. "Your preceptor?"

"You know, Karen. She's the nurse I follow around so I can learn how everything's done."

"Right, I remember now. I hope she's okay."

"She'll be fine, and you know, I'm really sorry she's sick. She's been so wonderful to work with, and she doesn't make me feel like an idiot all the time, but I wish she didn't have to be sick right now. It's thrown off my whole schedule."

"Oh, sweetheart."

There was a loud and decidedly unladylike sniffle from the telephone. "Anyway, I was running out of clean underwear, so I had to do some laundry, and I fell asleep sitting on the floor in front of the dryer in the dorm basement."

Maggie almost laughed, imagining her poor, worn-out little girl sound asleep in the laundry room. Then she felt like crying. To calm herself, she ran her fingers through Snickers's thick fur, getting a contented and comforting purr in return. "I'm sorry you're having such a rough time."

There was another long sniff. "And I slept right through my physiology exam this morning. Now I'm going to fail."

"They won't let you make it up?"

"Well," Emily admitted, "I can take the test that the professor's other class will take next week, but he'll deduct ten points right off the top for being late."

"It's better than failing, isn't it?"

"Yeah, I guess." Emily blew her nose. "But I have tests in psychology and English that day too. Why do I need more English? I want to be a nurse, not a writer."

"I guess they want you to be able to write up a report that people can read and understand."

"I can do that already. It's just something else to drive me crazy. How am I supposed to get everything done? And how am I supposed to do this for another three years? Mom, I can't do it."

"You *can*. I know what you're made of, Emily. You've got this."

Maggie wanted more than anything to be with her daughter, to wrap her baby girl in her arms and make everything okay. But she wasn't there. And Emily needed more than comfort.

"So can I come back home? Please, Mom?"

"You know I sold the cottage. Neither of us can go back there." Maggie assumed her daughter was referring to the cozy home they'd had in Vermont with Maggie's late husband, Richard.

"But you have lots of room in Somerset Harbor. Aunt Evelyn's house is huge." There was a sudden excitement in Emily's voice. "I could move in with you and work at the shop."

"What?"

"It'd be great! You need help there, don't you? I'm sure I could do it."

"Emily—"

"Really, Mom, it's the perfect solution. You'll have to teach someone the family business eventually, right? Why not me?"

"But what about your nursing career?"

"I don't want to be a nurse anymore." Once more there was a sob in Emily's voice.

Maggie ached to tell her to come home, that she could live at Sedgwick Manor for the rest of her life and work behind the counter at the shop and never have to worry about anything.

But she wouldn't be much of a mom if she did.

"Sweetie, you've wanted to be a nurse since you were a little girl. You've worked hard to get this far. You did fantastic in your classes last semester. I doubt you really want to give it all up now."

"Mom, you don't understand. I can't do it. The classes are harder this semester. I'm not smart enough, and I'm not good enough. I can't keep up."

"You certainly are smart enough," Maggie said, with a bit of sternness in her voice. "And you're good enough."

"I can't even wake up in time to get to class."

"So you messed up once. Do you think you're the only one? Do you think Clara Barton never missed a class?"

"Mom," Emily said in a tone that was generally accompanied by an eye roll.

"Do you think Florence Nightingale never fell asleep in front of the dryer?"

"Now you're being silly," Emily protested, but Maggie could tell she was also trying not to laugh.

"The point is that they didn't do everything perfectly all the time. But when they messed up, they figured out how to fix it and went on. And think of the terrible things they had to get through—the awful conditions, the lack of food and supplies and medicines, the idea that decent women shouldn't be near battlefields, caring for the sick and wounded. In spite of all that, they did what they knew they were made to do and changed the practice of medicine forever."

Emily sniffled. "Yeah, I guess you're right."

"You need to do what you were made to do, Emily. I can't decide what that is for you. If you're sure it's not nursing, then I suppose now's the time to realize that and cut your losses. And you know you can stay here until you figure out what is right for you."

Maggie waited for a response, but it didn't come right away. Snickers rubbed his head against her hand in a not-so-subtle hint for her to keep petting him.

"No," Emily said finally. "I guess I don't really think that. It's that—well, everything's so *hard*."

"And it ought to be, don't you think? It's not like running the register at the shop, you know. If I make a mistake with somebody's change, that's easy enough to fix. But if a nurse makes a mistake with someone's medicine or treatment, it could mean the difference between life and death. It's not a job just anyone should be doing. It takes a special kind of calling, a special kind of person who'll be dedicated to taking care of people. A special kind of person like you, sweetheart."

There was a brief pause on the other end before Emily asked in a tiny voice, "But what if I mess up again?"

"Then you do what you can to fix it and move on. You can't let one little thing that's hard to do stop you from being the person you want to be."

Emily sighed. "I suppose it wouldn't be much of an accomplishment if it was easy."

"Right now you're exhausted and upset. Of course everything seems awful. But I bet if you get a good night's sleep and then study hard all week, you'll see it's not as bad as you think."

"Well, I was ready for the test. I guess I'll be twice as ready with an extra week to study."

"Exactly," Maggie said, pleased to hear a fresh note of confidence in her daughter's voice.

"And usually there are some extra credit questions on the tests too."

Maggie smiled. "So you could still make an A even with the late penalty."

"Yeah, maybe."

"You can, sweetie. I know you can."

"You're my mom," Emily said, laughing softly. "You have to say that."

"No, I say that because I know you. I've seen how hard you work, and I know how much you really want this."

"I hate it when you're right."

"We have to do what makes us happy. You know I love the shop. I can't imagine anything better than getting to buy and sell antiques and find out about their histories and meet the people who own them. But that's me. You were meant for something more important."

"Your work is important too, Mom. You help a lot of people, but in a different way."

Maggie chuckled. "I don't exactly save people's lives, but I guess I do help them. Sort of. There was a girl at the shop today who looked like she needed help."

"What was the matter?"

"I'm not really sure. She said she wasn't in trouble, but she said it in a way that made me think she was."

"What did she come in for?"

"She had an antique ring to sell." Maggie described the pirate ring. "There was an inscription inside the band." She tried to pronounce the Latin. "*Conrigi vix tandem quod curvom est factum crede.*"

"What's that mean?" Emily asked. "No, wait a minute. Let me see. *Curvom.* 'Curved?' *Crede* is 'believe.' Ugh. I don't know enough Latin."

"I don't know any Latin, so I looked it up. It means, 'Believe you that what has once been made crooked can hardly now be made straight.'"

"That's more confusing than the Latin," Emily protested.

"I think what it means is that once something—or someone, I suppose—goes the wrong way, there's no chance it can be put right again."

"That's a pretty depressing sentiment, isn't it?"

"It is. I like to think anyone can choose to be better if he wants to. Sure there will probably be consequences for bad choices, but it seems like a good idea to stop making the bad choices at some point so the consequences don't keep piling up. As your dad used to say, 'When you find yourself in a hole, the first thing to do is stop digging.'"

Emily giggled.

"Now, speaking of good choices," Maggie said, "a few minutes ago, somebody mentioned you getting a good night's sleep."

"You're right. I'd better go to bed and get rested up." Emily groaned. "It all seems so overwhelming. Three tests?"

"You don't have to take three tests, honey."

"Huh?"

"You don't have to take three tests," Maggie repeated. "You just have to take one test. And then another test. And then another one. You remember how to eat an elephant, right?"

"Not Dad again."

"Come on, peanut," Maggie said in her best Richard voice. "How do you eat an elephant?"

Emily snickered. "One bite at a time."

"That's right. Take one thing at a time. You can do it. I don't have the slightest doubt."

"Thanks, Mom." Emily was silent for a moment, and then her voice was wistful. "I wish you were here."

Tears stung Maggie's eyes, but she didn't let them show in her voice. "Me too, but you don't need me. You're doing fine, and I am so proud of you. And I want you to call me after your last test is over and let me know how it all went."

"Yeah, okay."

"Promise?"

Emily laughed, a soft, sniffly kind of sound. "I promise."

"All right, honey. Sweet dreams. I love you."

"Love you too, Mom."

The connection ended, and Maggie sat for a moment, absently stroking the still-purring cat. *She'll be all right. It's only school. She's not sick or hurt or in real trouble. Please, God, be with her when I can't be, and help her sleep well tonight.*

She exhaled, feeling more relaxed, and then she thought about the girl who had come to the shop earlier that day. Gail wasn't much like Emily . . . but then again, she was. Did she have someone to go to for help? Someone to confide in? Someone who would guide her in the right direction? Despite her protestations, the girl had seemed troubled, even a little desperate. Maggie closed her eyes again and hugged Snickers as tightly as he would let her.

And please, Lord, take care of Gail Lee, whatever trouble she's in.

3

"**D**id you hear from Emily?" June asked as they opened the shop two days later. "You said you were worried about her."

"Oh, not worried. Not really," Maggie said. "Well, no more worried than any other mother of a teenage girl away from home for the first time."

June grinned.

"Anyway, Emily called again last night. Of course she hasn't taken her tests yet, but she slept really well the night we talked and feels more calm and confident now." Maggie's mouth turned down. "Every time I think of Emily, I can't help but think about the girl I bought the ring from."

"She hasn't called or come back," June said glumly. "I didn't think she would."

Maggie sighed. "At least we have the ring."

"Until the police come pick it up because someone reports it stolen."

"Aren't you Little Mary Sunshine?" Maggie said, making a silly face. "I did talk to Robert Linton about it late yesterday, and he says the police department doesn't have any information about a ring like that. He checked reports for the whole state."

June didn't look convinced. "Just because the police don't know about it doesn't mean it's not stolen. It apparently hasn't been reported yet."

"Well, he knows where to find it if he does get a report like that. In the meantime, I'm going to put it in the case. It's not for sale yet but for display. Maybe someone will come in and recognize it."

"It'd be a long shot," June said, "but I guess it wouldn't hurt to try. When I have a minute, though, I'm going to try researching it again. There are bloggers in town who specialize in local history. I tried some of their contact pages yesterday, and I'll check in with a few more today. I'll be in the back if you need me."

"Good idea. I'll talk to Ruth Harper too. The historical society ought to know something, especially if the ring belonged to someone from the area."

· · · · · · · · · · · · · · · · · ·

The next two days flew by, and the ring proved to be as much of a mystery as its owner. With June's help, Maggie had tried to track down any information about who might have owned the ring and how Gail Lee might have come to have it in her possession, but she'd come up empty. And as June had suspected, there weren't any Lees in Somerset Harbor and no Gail Lees in any of the surrounding towns.

Maggie had brought her laptop to the shop with her that morning so she could research during any slow periods. She had to tear herself away from her Internet search of *Maine coast pirates* when the bell on the shop door jingled.

"Good morning," she said, offering a pleasant smile to the man who came in. "Is there something I can help you with?"

He was in his midthirties, stocky, and not much taller than Maggie, and his pale skin was a sharp contrast to his lank black hair and mustache. She wasn't quite sure if the stubble on his chin was an attempt at being fashionable or a sign of laziness, but he wore a very expensive watch.

"Good morning," he said with a display of large, square teeth in a wide, catfish mouth. "I thought I'd have a look around if that's all right."

"Oh, certainly. Take your time. If you have any questions, let me know."

He nodded and started walking around the shop, pausing briefly here and there to examine a particular object and then moving on without touching it. She went back to her computer screen, but she kept track of him out of the corner of her eye.

She had almost reached the end of the mostly useless search results when she realized he had stopped in front of the jewelry display. He had his back to her, so she couldn't tell exactly what had caught his interest, but she was certain he was right in front of the pirate ring. She pretended to concentrate on the screen for a moment more, but he showed no sign of moving. *Maybe he knows something about the piece.* She could only hope.

"Isn't that one fascinating?" she asked as she moved to the part of the counter with the display case and stood across from him. "Would you like to see it?"

"If it's no trouble," he said, and though his voice was rather blasé, she could see a glimmer of excitement in his black eyes.

"No trouble at all."

She spread out the piece of black velvet they used to show their jewelry and set the ring on it. He hesitated for a moment before picking it up, one corner of his mouth turned up as he studied it. For a while he did nothing more. Then he began examining it more closely, holding it up to the light, squinting at the emerald set in it, and running his thumb over the bas-relief skeleton around the band. He took a magnifying glass from his pocket and studied the inscription on the inside of the ring, nodding as he read it.

"What do you want for it?" he asked finally.

Maggie narrowed her eyes. "You know this ring, don't you?"

He shrugged. "Maybe. At least it's possible I've heard of it. So what's the price?"

"It's only on display right now, but if it becomes available, I can let you know. If you'd like to leave your name and phone number, Mr. . . . ?"

"Oh, it's Peters, Edmund Peters. I'm a journalist, and I write a popular blog called *History's a Mystery*. This ring will be of interest to my readers."

"Nice to meet you, Mr. Peters." Maggie offered her hand. "I'm Maggie Watson. Evelyn Bradbury was my aunt."

"Right." He briefly shook her hand and then turned his attention to the ring again. "I bought some things from her over the years. Always fair. Always reasonable. Now, about this ring, I'd like to know who brought it in."

"I'm sorry, but that's confidential. The owner might not want to sell after all. We're trying to get some information about the ring so we can make a reasonable offer. Maybe you can help us with that. What have you heard about it?"

There was something sly about his grin. "Couldn't really say for sure. But I would like to have it, to help me check it out further."

Clearly he knew something. Now she was more determined than ever to find out where the ring had come from.

"Well, for now, it's not ours to sell." She kept her voice light but firm. "I can take down your phone number in case it becomes available, but that's the best I can do."

He grudgingly gave her his number, and she jotted it down on the top page of her clipboard.

"I'll give you $1,000 for it," he said. "Cash."

She couldn't hold back a bit of a chuckle. "Now you and I both know it's worth much more than that. And even if it weren't, it's still not for sale. I'm sorry, but there's really nothing I can do about it until I hear from the owner."

His wide mouth turned down.

"I will keep your number," she said, holding out her hand. "And I promise I'll call you if it becomes available."

He spent a defiant moment examining the ring again, and then he set it on her upturned palm.

"You do that."

Without another word, he stalked out of the shop.

. . . .

"I don't suppose you've had anyone ask about the ring yet," June said as she and Maggie took a well-deserved coffee break during a moment of calm the next morning.

"No one but Mr. Peters. We've had a few lookers. Several who wanted to try it on. Nobody who recognized it." Maggie took a sip of her coffee. "Any response from your local history bloggers?"

"He was one of the ones I contacted, actually," June said. "Peters. Normally I'd steer clear of that one, but I thought it was worth a shot."

"Ah. I suppose that's why he came in. I think he knows something about the ring, but he's certainly not saying."

June looked faintly disgusted. "Probably saving it for one of his 'big reveals,' as he calls them."

"Oh, yes. He said something about the ring being 'of interest' to his readers."

"He writes a lot of sensational stuff, minimally researched and then slanted to cause the most controversy. He used to write for the paper, but if I remember correctly, he got them sued a few years back, and they cut ties. I think he's happier this way though. No one to answer to."

"Hmm. Sounds like a nice guy."

"A real peach."

"Have you heard back from anyone else?"

June shook her head and took a sip of coffee. "Either nothing or regrets. Several of them suggest the ring might have belonged to a seafaring man, maybe a pirate." She rolled her eyes.

Maggie snorted. "Very helpful."

"Some gave me the names of pirates known to have sailed up and down the Maine coast, but nobody's heard of a ring like this one." The phone rang, and June took another quick sip of coffee. "I'll get it." She picked up the phone. "Carriage House Antiques. How may I help you? . . . Oh, Mrs. Ravenhurst, how are you? . . . Yes, I believe it came in this morning. Let me make sure."

Still chatting with the customer, June disappeared into the back of the shop. With a sigh, Maggie looked at the stack of antique sheet music she had arranged that morning for a display with a harpsichord. Two women had *oohed* and *aahed* over the titles and the decorative pages, each making a stack of her favorites. They ended up buying nothing and leaving a mess. But there was nothing to do except get it taken care of. She had just started sorting when the bell at the front door jingled, and Edmund Peters sauntered in.

"Mr. Peters. Good morning."

"Mrs. Watson." He graced her with a smarmy smirk. "I was hoping to have another look at that ring, if it's not too much trouble."

"If you like," she said, trying not to sound too indulgent. "But I'm afraid I still haven't heard from the owner about whether or not it's available for sale."

"Yes, I understand. I only wanted to see it again. Verify some details and all that. You don't mind, do you?"

"No, not at all."

Maggie spread out the square of black velvet once more and set the ring on it. She couldn't blame him for his interest in it. In the absence of any actual facts, she had come up with several tales about the man who would've worn such an unusual piece of jewelry. He may have been a villain, a thief, a rogue, and a conscienceless murderer, but she very much doubted that he had been dull.

"I wish you'd tell me what you know about it," she said. "I'm sure it's got an amazing history."

"Ah-ah-ah." He wiggled one thick finger at her. "If you think there's something special about it, you'll jack up the price on me. I know how it is." He planted both hands on top of the counter. "Tell me the truth now. This mysterious seller is all made up, right? To make the merchandise a little more unobtainable? A little more attractive?"

She managed to keep smiling. "Not at all. Though if you'd share what you know about it with us, that might help us decide on a price that's fair to everyone. If it does become available, I'd be very happy to contact you first to see if—"

She broke off as the doorbell jingled again. When the door opened, Maggie saw an elderly lady, tall and elegant, her perfectly white hair done up in a smooth chignon. Her jewelry was simple and understated but looked to be of the finest quality, just like the charcoal-colored linen jacket and slacks she wore and her gray leather handbag. Despite her age, her movements were so graceful and poised that Maggie wondered if a celebrity had entered the shop.

The woman caught Maggie's gaze, gave a slight nod, and said grandly, "Good morning. I am here to see June. Is she available?"

"Ah . . . yes, she is," Maggie said, stumbling over her words. "I'll get her for you."

Maggie turned back to Mr. Peters. "Excuse me for a moment, Mr. Peters." She picked up the ring and began to return it to the display case, but then set it back down as June appeared from the back of the shop.

"Good morning, Mrs. Ravenhurst! You certainly got here quickly. If you'd like to come this way, I'll let you see the chair for yourself. We haven't done more than unpack it, but I think you'll be very pleased."

Mrs. Ravenhurst glanced at the ring, then fixed a cool stare on Mr. Peters. After a moment, she followed June into the back of the shop.

Maggie stared after them but then caught herself. "I'm so sorry," she said, turning back to her customer.

Mr. Peters stood there, still with both hands flat on the top of the counter, staring at the gold-and-emerald ring glimmering on the square of velvet between them. "So what do you say? I'll give you $1,500, no questions asked."

"Mr. Peters, you know I can't do that." Maggie hoped she didn't sound as exasperated as she felt. "Even if the owner decides to sell right away, I don't think I'll be ready to part with it until I know more about it."

"I suppose I can understand that." He held up his hands. "I guess there's nothing else I can do."

"I'll keep in touch if there's any news."

He nodded with a hint of a defeat. "Please do."

He turned to leave and almost knocked over June and Mrs. Ravenhurst as they came out of the back of the shop.

"Oh!" June exclaimed.

"Sorry," he said, ducking his head. "I didn't see you there."

"Goodness." June placed one hand over her heart. "I didn't see you either. Are you all right, Mrs. Ravenhurst?"

"Yes, certainly." The older woman lifted one silvery eyebrow and regarded Peters rather icily.

He merely smirked in return, bid them all good morning, and strode out of the shop.

"I'm so sorry," June told her client when he was gone. "I should have been paying better attention."

"There was no harm done." Mrs. Ravenhurst glanced back

at the jewelry display and then turned again to June. "Now, as I was telling you, I think the chair is perfect, but I would rather have a pair. If you can find another, that would be excellent. If not, perhaps you can find a different pair in the same style."

"I'll see what I can do," June said with a smile. "Before you go, I'd like to introduce you to the owner of the shop, Maggie Watson. Evelyn Bradbury was her aunt."

"How do you do, Mrs. Ravenhurst?" Maggie came around the jewelry counter and held out her hand. "June tells me you're interested in furniture from the Queen Anne period."

Mrs. Ravenhurst grasped Maggie's hand lightly. "I am." She nodded at Maggie and let go. "My home was built when the style began to be popular here, and since I'm having some restorations done, I thought I would bring in some additional pieces to enhance the period feel."

"The Ravenhurst home is nearly three hundred years old," June said.

"Built in 1722," Mrs. Ravenhurst added, her smile serene. "The first Ravenhurst in Somerset Harbor had it built for his young bride, and there has never been a time in all the years since that a Ravenhurst hasn't lived there."

"I've heard it's lovely," Maggie said. "What a history it must have."

"We were one of the first families here, you know, and go back to Edward Fuller off the *Mayflower*. I couldn't very well furnish my home from Ikea."

At first Maggie thought the older woman had meant to be amusing. Then, from her disdainful expression, she thought Mrs. Ravenhurst might be deadly serious. To be safe, Maggie merely nodded.

"We're happy to help you find anything you need to make your home look as historically authentic as possible."

"Excellent." Mrs. Ravenhurst took a pair of sunglasses from her handbag. "Let me know what you find out about the chairs, June."

June nodded. "Of course. I have a good lead from a source in Portland."

"Very good. And if you can find a genuine tilt-top tea table, I'd be very interested. In excellent condition, of course."

"Right."

"Nice to meet you, Ms. Watson," Mrs. Ravenhurst said.

"Call me Maggie. We hope to see you again soon." Maggie hurried to open the door.

Mrs. Ravenhurst passed out of the shop like a queen. "I'll be back."

Maggie held her breath until the door was firmly shut. Then she blinked at June. "If that's not local royalty, I don't know what is."

"No doubt about it," June said with a grin. "And she'd be the first to let you know."

They went back behind the cash register and sat down.

"She seems awfully proud of a family she married into," Maggie said. "Though I guess she's been a Ravenhurst for a long time now."

"Oh, all her life. She was born a Ravenhurst. And since she was an only child, she had her husband take the Ravenhurst name too."

"Wow," Maggie said. "She's serious about it."

"Yeah, it never sat well with him. I think he left, but I can't be sure. It would have happened before I was born, and people simply don't talk about him."

Maggie's eyes widened. "I hope she had sons."

"One son, but he's passed on. And the son had two girls, both of them married to men not named Ravenhurst."

Maggie snickered. "Uh-oh."

"Yeah," June said. "Evidently none of that fit in with her plans for carrying on the Ravenhurst name, so now she seems determined to see the mansion itself returned to its former glory."

"I bet she has some interesting family stories she could tell. Maybe I'll get brave enough to ask her someday."

June frowned. "Well, drat. I should have asked her if she knows anything about that ring of yours. Evidently her family had a run-in with some pirates generations ago, before the first Ravenhurst arrived in Somerset Harbor. You should have her tell you about it if you get a chance. It's quite a tale."

"I'll do that. But I'd like you to tell me the history between her and Peters. The look she gave him could have killed fifty people."

"I don't blame her," June said, looking rather angry. "When he still worked for the paper, he'd planned to publish something unseemly about the Ravenhursts that he dug up from I-don't-know-where. Something about a Ravenhurst being a bootlegger long ago. Mrs. Ravenhurst found out and had the story killed."

Maggie raised her eyebrows. "Was that what he got fired for?"

"No, that was right before. He got fired for writing something different, though I can't remember about what or whom. But by then the paper had had enough of him and sent him packing. I have a feeling Mrs. Ravenhurst applied a little pressure then too."

"But what did he know about the Ravenhurst bootlegger?"

June shrugged. "I never heard the whole story, but I guess he figured it wasn't worth the trouble he'd catch if he spread it around town on the sly."

Maggie shook her head. "He can obviously keep his mouth shut when he wants to."

"Now, don't give up." June stood and gave Maggie's shoulder a pat. "I'll make us some fresh coffee. Then I'll go see what I can find in mint-condition Queen Anne armchairs while you dig for treasure about local pirates."

Maggie brought the mystery ring to the next meeting of the Somerset Harbor Historical Society. She had already grown to love the Victorian home—painted pale rose and teal with abundant gingerbread trim—where the meetings were held, as well as the ladies who made up the society itself. By the time Maggie arrived, the house's formal dining room was already lively with chatter and the clink of cups and cookie plates.

"Maggie!" Daisy Carter patted the empty chair beside her at the long table, her blue eyes especially bright. "You sit right here, honey. I want to see this pirate ring you've got."

"We don't exactly know that it's a pirate ring at this point," Maggie said as she sat down.

Ina Linton, the oldest member of the society, put her hands on her hips, the cotton fluff of her sparse pin curls reminding Maggie of a banty hen with her feathers ruffled. "You calm down now, Daisy. Let her settle for a minute. How about some refreshments, Maggie?"

"That would be great."

Liz Young, the pastor's wife, passed her a cup and the cookie plate. "My mother's recipe. Nobody made down-home oatmeal raisin cookies like she did."

"Ooh." Maggie took one and bit into it, then closed her eyes. "Heavenly. Thank you."

"Come on, Maggie," Daisy urged. "Can't you eat cookies and show us the ring at the same time?"

June grinned at Daisy, then turned to Maggie. "I made the mistake of repeating your Jack Sparrow comment to her. Now she thinks if she rubs the ring and says the magic word, Johnny Depp is going to appear from nowhere."

Daisy patted her well-teased brunet hair and drawled in her charming Southern accent, "I can't say I'd mind if he did."

"Let's deal with reality," Ruth Harper said, giving Daisy a reproving stare over the top of her glasses. As the president of the historical society, she knew how to take charge. "Why don't you show us this ring, Maggie, and we'll go from there."

Maggie brought a ring box out of her purse and set it on the polished table in front of her. With every eye on her, she opened it to reveal the glimmering gold and emerald of the ring. There was a chorus of *oohs* and *aahs* from around the table.

"Wow," Daisy breathed. "Even I wouldn't wear something that big."

Maggie chuckled. "Pretty impressive, isn't it?"

"And you don't know anything about it at all?" Fran Vosburg was usually quiet, listening to the others talk, but now she leaned forward so she could see the ring better. "This whole design is very interesting. Almost overwhelming."

Being younger than the rest of the members of the historical society and not a native of Somerset Harbor, Fran usually deferred to the other ladies, but since she owned The Quilt Cupboard and had a degree in design, Maggie thought her insight might make her especially helpful in this case.

"Anything else you particularly notice about the design?" Maggie asked, handing it to her.

Fran shrugged and turned faintly pink. "*Overwhelming* is the best word I have for it. Judging by the amount of gold in the ring and the size of that emerald, whoever had this made wanted everyone to know he was very rich. And judging by the sea serpent and the cutlasses and the skeleton, he also wanted everyone to know he was very dangerous."

"What does the inscription say?" Ina asked, her eyes sparkling with interest.

Daisy took the ring, squinting as she scanned the inside of the band. "*Con . . . rigi vix tandem*—huh?"

"Basically it means once you've gone wrong, you can never expect to get back on the right path," Maggie said.

Liz chuckled softly. "So besides letting everyone know he was rich and dangerous, he didn't want them to expect him to ever change his wicked ways. The owner of this ring must have been quite a character."

"Let me see it," Ruth said.

"I hope you can make more sense out of that mumbo jumbo than I can," Daisy said, handing the ring to her.

Ruth pulled her glasses down slightly farther on her nose and studied the ring for a long moment. "I can't help thinking I've seen a sea serpent like that before. Not on a ring but on something else. I wish I could remember where."

"I wish you could too," Maggie said. "I was hoping it belonged to a local pirate, or at least someone who sailed mostly along the Maine coast, but I didn't find anything the least bit helpful. June and I—"

Ruth snapped her fingers. "Zane."

"What?"

"Wait a minute." Ruth disappeared into the corridor and came back a few minutes later carrying two books, a large one that looked at least a hundred years old and a very small one with a clasp on it that must have been older still.

"Solomon Zane, Somerset Harbor's very own pirate legend." She put the books on the table and opened the larger of the two, quickly flipping through the pages. "He's not that well-known outside the area, but he does have a mention in this book about eighteenth-century history." She stopped scanning. "There."

She settled on a page with an etching of a ship. Below it was a close-up drawing of the flag that flew from the mast, and on it was a sea serpent wrapped around the globe, like the sea serpent that was wrapped around the emerald in the ring. There was no mistaking it.

Maggie leaned over the book, her heart racing as she read aloud, "'*The Leviathan sailed the Maine coast under the lawless murderer Solomon Zane until he came to his deserved end.*'"

On the facing page, with the simple inscription *Solomon Zane*, was a drawing of a man wearing what could only be described as stereotypical pirate garb—the long coat with brass buttons, high boots, a tricorne hat, and a ruffled shirt. His curly hair and beard were black, long, and unkempt, and he had a pistol in one hand and a cutlass in the other. But there was something generic about the face depicted there. It seemed unlikely that the artist had ever seen Zane or heard a description of him.

Maggie turned to the next page, scanning it until she found the name again.

> *The coast was plagued by these seafaring highwaymen, including the notorious Solomon Zane, thought to have come to these waters from his native Cornwall. He pillaged the coast of Maine for some twenty years, engaging in kidnapping, murder, and all manner of piracy on land and on sea until a just Providence ended his reign of terror in 1720. In that time, trade in fishing, lumbering, and shipbuilding—*

The rest was about the economy and population. Frowning, Maggie turned to the page before the etching of the ship. "Ruth, isn't there anything else about him in here?"

"It's not very helpful, I know," Ruth said, but then she

patted the smaller book. "There's not a lot in here either, but there is more."

"A diary?"

Ruth shook her head regretfully. "I wish it was, but it's more a notebook of sorts. I've been meaning to gather up what we have on Zane and put it on the society website. If I had done it years ago, you might not have had such a hard time finding out something about that ring."

"Unless there's something in there that mentions a huge ring with a sea serpent on it, it probably wouldn't have made any difference."

"No," Ruth said with a chuckle. "Nothing like that. And even in here there's not all that much. Most of it is about local happenings—new businesses, deaths, births—but there are some clippings from the newspaper that was printed roughly once a month. There are three mentions of Zane, if I remember right. Once was from when he sank an English frigate in the harbor, about 1710 or '11. Then there was the time he kidnapped the daughter of the wealthiest man in town. The last was when the girl came back home and Zane disappeared."

"What happened to him?" Maggie asked, intrigued.

"A couple of us have had a few chats about that over coffee, haven't we, girls?"

The other women laughed.

"I think the girl's family got him," Ina said fiercely. "Serves him right."

June helped herself to a cookie. "I guess I must have missed those chats. I mean, I've heard of him, but I don't remember us talking about him."

"It's been a while," Ruth told her. "And you may not have been in on all of them."

"Still," June said, "Mrs. Ravenhurst was in the shop recently, and that should have reminded me of him."

Maggie blinked. "Wait. This Solomon Zane is the pirate her ancestors had the run-in with before they were Ravenhursts?"

"The very same," Ruth said.

Maggie looked at the women gathered around the dining table. "Do you really think they . . . *got rid* of him?"

"Could be."

Maggie picked up the ring, turning it over yet again. "If this did belong to Solomon Zane, notorious pirate, how in the world did Gail Lee end up with it?"

Daisy pursed her red lips. "Who's Gail Lee?"

"She's the one who brought in the ring," Maggie said, her worry about the girl returning.

"I was telling her I don't know of any Lees in the area." June eyed the other ladies at the table.

"I sure don't know any," Daisy said. "And I usually at least hear about everyone in the area when I'm working at The Busy Bean."

"And David and I usually visit any newcomers," Liz said. "There hasn't been anyone by that name. What was she like?"

"Sixteen or seventeen, I'd say." Maggie frowned, thinking. "Very slim, blond hair that tends to hang in her face, dark eyes. She seemed a little shy but got kind of defensive when I asked her if she was in trouble."

June shook her head. "I still don't think we'll see her again. She was in too big of a hurry to get some money, no matter how much."

"Did you give her money, Maggie?" Ruth asked with concern.

"Five hundred," Maggie said, suddenly feeling as if she were the biggest nincompoop in the world. "I figured the ring had to be worth much more than that and she'd be back. And I really wanted to help her."

"She didn't say why she needed the money, did she?"

Liz asked. "Maybe you should have had her come talk to me and David."

"I don't think she would have gone to see a pastor, to be honest," Maggie said, smiling at her friend. Liz, a counselor as well as the pastor's wife, was always ready to lend a hand and an ear.

"I think the best thing you could do at this point, Maggie, is have the ring examined by an expert." Ruth looked unsettled. "There are some awfully good artificial stones now. It wouldn't be easy to spot one of those right off."

"I'm pretty sure the stone and the gold are real. And the girl said she didn't know anything about the ring itself, except that it had been in her family for a long time."

"You didn't get a telephone number or an address?" Ina asked.

Maggie nodded. "An address, at least. And a driver's license number. But I was too concerned about her to ask for more. I was afraid that if I pressed her, she'd take off with the ring. I thought she'd at least come back for it or for more money or something."

"I think you'd better get this authenticated and appraised," Ruth said, her expression still grim. "I hate to think you could have been taken advantage of."

"I don't suppose you know of anyone qualified to authenticate something like this," Maggie said hopefully. "I tried to call Nigel Holman, that gemologist who helped us with the key a few months ago, but he's out of the country for the next three weeks."

"Pop could do it," Daisy piped up.

Ruth nodded. "I think he's just the one. He might even be able to tell you a little more about Solomon Zane, or at least about the pirate activity around Somerset Harbor back in the day. If anyone's an expert on local pirate lore, it's Pop."

Maggie's forehead wrinkled. "Who's he?"

"He was my history teacher when I was a freshman in high school, believe it or not," Ina said with an impish grin. "Between what he knows and what Willa Ravenhurst knows, I doubt there's anything else you can find out about Zane. And it might be precious little even then. Anyway, his real name is Samuel Welborn, but folks around here mostly call him Pop."

Maggie bit back a laugh, trying to imagine how old this "Pop" must be if he'd taught seventy-something Ina when she was a girl.

"Is he—is he doing okay?"

That made Ina crow with laughter. "You sound like anyone over fifty must have one foot in the grave."

Maggie's face felt slightly warm. "Well, I just thought he must be getting a bit older by now and—"

"He does at least as well as I do, I'd say, and I get along pretty well. To hear him tell it, he's fine, if you don't make him walk too far or too fast."

"That's great," Maggie told her. "I'd certainly love to have a talk with him and let him look at the ring."

"I should have thought of him in the first place," June said. "He's examined a few things for the society, but it's been a while."

Ruth looked thoughtful for a minute. "You know, Maggie, the last time I checked, and I admit it was years ago, there was almost nothing available on the Internet about Zane. We might want to see what's out there now. And after we collect all the information we can find, we should use it to write up an article for the society website. It would add some color, and the little mystery about what happened to the old rogue might stir up some interest in Somerset Harbor and the society. It would be wonderful to have that ring photographed to put with the article *if* it turns out to be Zane's ring. What do you think? Would you be up to writing that, Maggie?"

"That's a great idea," Liz chimed in.

Fran nodded enthusiastically. "You could contact other sites that feature pirate history and offer to let them link to the story."

"I'm not much of a writer, but I'd love to give it a try." Maggie held up a hand to quell the excited chatter her statement brought about. "*After* I find out if this is really his ring."

"And," Daisy added, "you could use a picture of Jack Sparrow as sort of an idea of what he might have looked like."

June shook her head. "Will you stop with Johnny Depp already?"

"I absolutely will not. He's the best actor in Hollywood."

Maggie chuckled and then turned to Ruth. "How do I get in touch with Pop?"

"He lives off Wharf Road past Cemetery Hill with his granddaughter, Dani Freemont. I'll have to look up the phone number and the address for you."

"You don't think he'd mind if I called him, do you, Ruth? Maybe you should talk to him first and let him know you sent me."

"Don't be silly," Ina said. "He'd love to tell to you about Zane. Everything he knows, anyway. Tell him the girls at the historical society gave you his name. Be prepared though. He'll talk your ear off if you let him."

"I won't mind that in the least." Maggie slipped the ring back into the black velvet ring box and put it in her purse. "For now, I want to keep it safe until we know more about it. I didn't like how that Mr. Peters was looking at it when he came into the shop."

Daisy frowned. "I swear, that man's like a shark with blood in the water. How'd he know to come for it?"

"I'm afraid that was my doing," June said. "I made the mistake of sending him an e-mail when Maggie first got the ring. I thought he might know something."

Maggie refilled her coffee cup. "I think he does. He wouldn't tell me anything, of course, but he definitely wanted the ring. He came in twice and made offers."

"You keep an eye on him anytime he's around," Ina said, pursing her lips. "Historian, my foot. Troublemaker, if you ask me."

"He didn't have a chance to do anything when he was there," Maggie assured her. "But if he comes back into the shop, I certainly won't let him out of my sight as long as the ring is on display."

5

Late the next morning, Maggie called the number Ruth had given her for Pop Welborn. His granddaughter answered the phone and told Maggie that Pop was taking part in a gathering for World War II vets in Washington, D.C. She offered Maggie his cell phone number, but Maggie decided she would wait until he was back in town and recovered from his travels before she bothered him.

The telephone at the shop rang the next evening, and Maggie was pleasantly surprised to find her caller was Pop Welborn himself.

"Dani told me you called," he said, his voice steady and clear. "Is there something I can help you with?"

She told him briefly about the ring. "I understand you're something of an expert about local pirate lore."

He chuckled. "'Expert' might be a stretch. But I have done some study on the early eighteenth century, especially in coastal Maine, and I've collected a few artifacts. Ruth Harper and the other ladies of the historical society have called on me a time or two to answer some questions. I think maybe Ina puts a little too much stock in my being a history teacher back during the Paleozoic era."

Maggie chuckled. "I'm sure she just appreciates that you know so many things."

"Well, that remains to be seen, young lady. Now when can I come see this prize of yours?"

"I wouldn't want to impose on you to come here," she said, reeling slightly from being called "young lady." "If it's all right, I thought I'd bring it to you, and then you can tell me whether or not it's authentic and what you know about Solomon Zane."

"I tell you what, it'll be just as easy for me to stop by your shop tomorrow after I go to the hospital."

The hospital? "No," Maggie said quickly. "I mean, I don't want you to worry about this at all. If you need to go to the hospital, I don't want to bother you with something as trivial as this ring. Oh, I'm sorry. I didn't know. Ina said you were doing fine, and your granddaughter didn't mention—"

The old man burst out laughing. "No no. There's nothing to be concerned about. I'm not ready for the churchyard yet. I have to go to the hospital for my regular blood test. This rat poison they have me on to keep my blood thinned out is tricky stuff, and they have to make sure it's thin enough but not too thin. It only takes about ten minutes to have them draw some blood, and then I can come by and have a chat with you. How would that be?"

She exhaled heavily. "If you're sure it's no trouble. You scared me for a minute there, Mr. Welborn."

"Now, you call me Pop like everybody else does, and we'll get along fine."

"All right . . . Pop. What time should I expect you?"

"If the hospital doesn't keep me waiting any longer than usual, I'd say about midafternoon. If it's going to be much later than that, I'll give you a call. How'd that be?"

"That'll be perfect." Maggie beamed, though he couldn't see her. "Absolutely perfect."

· · · · · · · · · · · · · · · · ·

Good as his word, Pop Welborn showed up at the antiques shop at two thirty the next afternoon. He was tall, spare, and a little stoop-shouldered, as if he had once been taller. He didn't look as if he could have been more than seventy or so, but he wore a cap with a ship embroidered on the front with *LST-118, 1943*. Even if he had been very young when he signed up, that would make him at least ninety or more.

"You must be Mrs. Watson," he said with a smile and a firm handshake.

"Call me Maggie, please. I'm so glad you could come."

Once they were settled in a pair of comfortable chairs with some hot coffee, he brought out a three-ring binder stuffed with papers, some of them yellowed with age, some bright white and brand-new. There were a few newspaper articles—some actual newsprint and some merely copies. There were also a few pieces of the old thermal paper once used for faxes and printing microfiche.

"You've been at this a long time," she said, and he gave her a wink.

"Gotta be good for something. I'm sorry I have to tell you, though, not all of this is about Solomon Zane. In fact, not much of it is. Why don't we start with what you know?"

She showed him the copies she had made from the books at the historical society. "And the ring, of course. I'll get it."

He patted her hand. "Let's save that for last, why don't we? Sort of the big finish."

"Sure." She flipped through the meager copies and notes she'd given him. "It's not much. I'd love to know more."

He opened the binder where one of several camouflage sticky notes marked the place. "I went through here last night so I wouldn't have to waste your time hunting for what I needed. You've already seen this picture of his ship and his flag, and the drawing of him."

"Do you think he came from Cornwall like the book says?"

"I've never heard anything to the contrary," Pop said, "and I did some e-mailing with some folks in my genealogical group who are over there. Their records do show a Solomon Zane born in Penryn, Cornwall, in 1663, presumably the same one who broke out of jail in 1690 and stowed away on a clipper ship bound for the South Seas. That ship was scuttled by pirates and all the crew presumed killed, but about five years later, a ship called *The Leviathan* started harrying ships down around Haiti. Eventually, it moved up our coast and started picking off English cargo ships and finally raiding the towns."

"And *The Leviathan* was captained by Solomon Zane!"

"Exactly," he said, gray eyes twinkling. "You get an A."

He let her browse the e-mails and copies of old clippings he had collected. No, there wasn't that much, but the supposition that the Zane who had escaped justice in Cornwall was the same one who had practiced piracy in Maine seemed a logical one.

"I guess there's no way to be absolutely sure," Maggie said, poring over one of the pages that traced the pirate's genealogy back three generations and forward only as far as a son named Remembrance. Zane's wife, Matilda, had died in 1697, the son in 1721. "Do you know what happened to his family?"

"I could never find much on the wife except she was also from Cornwall and died in Havana."

"And their son?"

"As best I can tell," Pop said, "he stayed with his mother's family after she died. But he was with Zane later on, until Zane disappeared in 1720. There was a fellow called Razor Drummond who served as Zane's first mate on *The Leviathan* when Zane first started his pirating. Drummond was listed as captain of the ship when it was captured by the British in 1721 and was hanged a month later. Most of the crew was killed when the ship was taken. It's assumed that Remembrance Zane was killed along with them, but his body was never found."

"What happened to Zane himself?"

"That's also something of a mystery." He flipped through the binder to a piece of lined notebook paper that had been written on with a ballpoint pen in a utilitarian script. "Have you talked to Mrs. Ravenhurst about Zane? I wrote down the story she tells about her family's involvement with Zane, but my notes are just the bare facts."

"I haven't had a chance to ask her yet," Maggie said. "But we're helping her procure some antiques to go along with the restoration work she's having done at her home, so I was going to bring it up the next time she came in."

"She makes a much better tale of it than I do," he admitted. "But from what she says, Thomas Lacey was the richest man in Somerset Harbor, and he had a young daughter named Caroline who was stolen out of her bed in the middle of the night. She was held for ransom on *The Leviathan* for two or three weeks."

"The poor girl. How did they get her back?"

"That's the strange part. Lacey managed to get enough cash together to pay what Zane asked, but before he could turn it over, the girl showed up back at home."

"How did she escape?"

"Nobody knew." He peered through thick glasses as he searched for another article in his binder. "This says she was so distraught from her experience that she couldn't tell them anything. She was evidently unharmed but so frightened that she blocked it all out."

Maggie took a large drink of her forgotten coffee and then made a face. "Ugh. Ice cold. Would you like a fresh cup?"

"If it's not too much trouble."

"It's no trouble at all."

She took his cup and her own, dumped out the contents, and quickly made a new pot of coffee. Then she hurried back to her chair.

"It'll be ready in a few minutes," she told her guest. "Anyway,

I thought Mrs. Ravenhurst's family had some kind of confrontation with Zane and rescued the girl. Is that not true?"

"Well, according to Mrs. Ravenhurst, the story passed down through the family is that the girl's father and brothers went after Zane, and from all accounts he was never seen or heard from after that time. Everyone assumes they killed him and disposed of the body."

Maggie arched a brow. "You don't sound so sure."

"I suppose it's possible. But I'm not sure how a middle-aged merchant and his two half-grown sons managed to do what the authorities in Somerset Harbor and the whole British navy couldn't without so much as a shot fired or a murmur from Zane's evidently formidable crew."

"Hmmm. Maybe the crew wanted him out of the way. Didn't you say his first mate took over the ship after Zane disappeared?"

"There is that, I suppose. But from all accounts, at least during the last of the time he sailed, Zane was generous with his crew and treated them well. They'd have no reason to betray him. And they had easy pickings, mostly due to the fear the local residents had of Zane himself. Without him leading them, they'd have had to work much harder."

The familiar ding of the coffeemaker sounded, and Maggie stood up.

"I'll get our coffee and the ring, if you're ready."

"Now would be good," Pop said.

Maggie poured the fresh coffee and brought the two cups to the table. "By the way, the historical society wants me to write a short article on Zane to put up on their website. Would it be possible for me to make copies of the information you have so I can use it in the article? I'd credit you, of course."

"No credit needed," Pop assured her. "And I figured you might want these." He handed her some papers that were loose in the back of his binder. They were copies of all the documents he had shown her.

"Oh, this is great!" She beamed at him. "This is so thoughtful of you and so helpful. Now, let me get the ring and you can tell me what you think."

She took the ring from the display case and brought it to him, watching the eager delight in his eyes.

"Well well." He turned it over in his hand and then touched one finger to the sea serpent that guarded the emerald. "That certainly looks like his insignia. Exactly like the flag he flew. My goodness."

As Peters had done, Pop rubbed his thumb over the bas-relief skeleton on the outside of the band and then squinted at the inscription inside.

"I'm afraid my Latin is pretty rusty, but I think I get the gist of it. You can't straighten out something that's gone crooked, right?"

"That's about it." Maggie took a breath. "What do you think?"

"It seems to be old." He jiggled the ring in his hand. "Feels heavy enough to be gold. But let's do some tests first."

He set a little kit bag on the table and took out a collection of small bottles, a black touchstone, and a jeweler's loupe. She watched as he used the ring to make several golden stripes across the touchstone.

"You want to be careful with this stuff," he said as he put a drop from each of the little bottles on its own stripe. "It's acid."

Maggie's eyes widened as she thought about what June had paid for the Duncan Phyfe table they were sitting at, but his hands were steady, and he was quick to seal up the bottles and return them to his bag. He peered at the touchstone for a moment, and then, without comment, studied the ring through the loupe.

After a moment, he put down the loupe. "The gold is plated and the emerald is green glass." With a sigh, he set the ring back on the table. "It's a very interesting creation and seems to point to Solomon Zane, but it's definitely a fake." He shook his head. "I'm sorry."

Maggie gaped at him. "Wh—what? No, that can't be right. I examined that emerald. I tested the gold."

"Well," he said soothingly, "some of these little tests can be misleading. And it can be hard to tell, even under magnification, if a stone—"

"No." She blinked hard, willing the frustrated tears to stay behind her eyes. "Look, I know it's not much of a test, but I did test it."

She scurried over to the drawer behind the counter and got the unglazed ceramic piece they used to test gold. There was still a glimmering mark on it from the last time she had used it. She grabbed the ring and rubbed it beneath the mark already there. Then the tears sprang into her eyes. The new mark was black.

"But the stone . . ."

She picked up the loupe he had brought with him and studied the supposed emerald. Under magnification, it looked nothing like it had before. She went back to the drawer and got the loupe she had used when Gail Lee brought the ring to her. It made no difference. The stone was definitely glass.

She swallowed hard. "This isn't the same ring."

6

"I'm so sorry," June said when she came back from the estate sale she had gone to that afternoon. She squeezed Maggie's arm. "I'm just . . . I'm so sorry."

"I can't understand it," Maggie said, tears stinging her eyes. "I'm *positive* the ring I got from Gail was real. It was at least real gold and a real emerald. I'm sure about that."

"I know." June gave her a sheepish little grin. "I checked it."

"You did? When?"

"The day you got it."

"Well, that's good to know. At least I'm not crazy." Maggie stared at the ring, which sparkled brightly, mocking her with its false grandeur.

"You're not crazy."

"Pop said this one is pretty old."

"Did he have any idea what century it's from?" June asked.

"Probably the middle of the nineteenth century. He thinks it's a copy of the original."

"But why? Who would make a copy of something like that unless it's for this sort of thing—selling it and then switching it out for a fake?"

"I don't know. He said sometimes women would have paste copies made of their finest jewels so they could wear them in public and not worry about them being stolen or lost."

"Clever."

Maggie nodded. "He thinks someone might have wanted to flash Zane's notorious pirate ring around town but keep the original locked up safe at the same time. I guess it's possible."

"I suppose," June said. "Reminds me of that story about the woman who borrowed her friend's priceless necklace and lost it. So she borrowed the money to have another one made and returned it to her friend without telling her what she'd done. Then, after working herself half to death for years to repay the debt, she found out the lost necklace was only a paste copy in the first place."

"Oh my. That's tragic." Maggie somehow dredged up a slight smile. "By the way, I checked the phone number for the address on Gail Lee's driver's license."

"No such address?" June asked. "Not a working telephone number?"

"It's a real address and a working number, but the people who have lived there for the past thirty-five years are named Martin."

"And I'll bet they've never heard of anyone called Gail Lee," June guessed.

"Unfortunately, no." "A fake ID," June said, nodding sagely. "I guess this is an expensive lesson about not trusting everybody who happens to look sweet and innocent."

"I still don't know about that." Maggie grimaced at the receipt Gail Lee had left for the $500 with an almost-childish scrawl for a signature. "She did leave an emerald ring here. She hasn't been back. How could she have switched it out for the fake one?"

June considered for a moment. "If this was a con, she would most likely have had someone working with her. She gives you her helpless little girl act and takes the cash, and her boyfriend or mother or whoever comes in later, admires the ring, and makes the switch when we aren't watching."

Maggie bit her lip. "I suppose that could be what happened, but I know you. You wouldn't have shown anyone something that valuable and that portable without keeping your eye on whoever it was. And you've made sure I do the same thing when I'm with a customer."

"Right. Are you sure you didn't get distracted when you were showing someone the ring?"

"I'm sure."

"Not even for a second?"

Maggie shook her head. "I didn't have many, and none of them were serious buyers. The only one who actually made me an offer—oh."

"What?"

Maggie winced. "It was when Mrs. Ravenhurst came in. She asked for you, and . . . I was about to put the ring back in the case and go get you, but then you came out to meet her. I couldn't have looked away from Peters for more than a few seconds. He had his hands on the counter with the ring sitting there between them. I didn't think he moved at all. He made me another offer for the ring after that. You don't think he could have . . . ?" She suddenly felt a little bit sick.

"I wouldn't put it past the little weasel," June said, "but I can't picture him being in on it with the girl in the first place. That seems out of character for him. He likes to think he's an expert on all things historical, and he likes his collection of artifacts, but he doesn't seem the type to run a scam like this for only $500."

"You're right," Maggie said, frowning. "I could see him wanting the ring for himself or wanting to be the one who publishes the story about Zane—probably with his own wild theory about why he disappeared—but I don't see why he'd go to all this trouble to skin me out of a few hundred dollars."

"Unless, after he came to see the ring, he had the fake one made so he could have the real one himself," June huffed. "No, that can't be right. Pop said the copy is at least a 150 years old, right? Hmmm. I don't know what to think."

"He probably wouldn't have had time to do something like that anyway. Besides, he didn't take any pictures or make notes. How could he have made such a perfect copy? No, as convenient as it would be to assume he had something to do with all this, I don't see how it's possible. That takes us back to Gail Lee."

June pressed her lips together. "I think you'd better report all this to Robert Linton. He'll know how to handle it."

Maggie didn't say anything for a minute. As foolish as it seemed, she still wanted to help Gail. She still couldn't believe there wasn't a good explanation for everything that had happened. "I don't think I'm ready to involve the police yet. I'd rather see what I can find out on my own."

June nodded, and then she gazed around the shop nervously. "What if . . . what if someone came in while we were closed and made the switch? It would have to be either the girl or someone working with her, but isn't that possible too?"

Maggie's eyes widened. "Very possible. But if someone did take the risk of breaking in to steal the ring, why replace it? And why not take more than that?"

"Maybe we'd better have a look around anyway. We might have missed something."

It was a slow afternoon anyway, so Maggie and June had plenty of time to check all the doors and windows in the shop for any sign of tampering. They also made sure nothing out on display was missing or out of place. Everything was as it should be.

"It must have happened while we were here," Maggie admitted. She put her elbow on the Duncan Phyfe table where she and Pop had sat earlier that day and leaned her chin on her hand. "It seems a strange thing to use for a scam though, doesn't it? Very specific to Somerset Harbor. Or at least to the

Maine coast. And how many 150-year-old copies of that ring could they have? It's not a very practical method of defrauding antiques shops."

June chuckled. "I always figured if criminals were really smart, they wouldn't be criminals."

"No, I suppose not. But it seems I'm not any smarter, falling for whatever this scheme is."

"It's all right," June said, patting her arm. "At least you didn't give the girl the whole value of the ring."

"True. And I'm not through with this yet. I *am* going to find out what's going on here."

. . . .

Maggie was more than exhausted when she went home that evening. She stared into the refrigerator to see what she might make for dinner, but cooking the chicken casserole she had planned seemed like too much trouble. The leftovers from her lasagna looked utterly disgusting, though she knew that had more to do with her state of mind than the actual quality of the food. It would be delicious warmed up—it always was—but she didn't feel like bothering with it.

She ended up making a peanut butter sandwich and then feeling nostalgic because she remembered how much Emily loved them. Snickers immediately jumped up into her lap when she sat at the table in the kitchen nook.

"I'm all right, silly." She scratched behind his ears and down his back, eliciting a deep, happy purr. "I'm not going to cry over something as foolish as this. I'm not." Snickers tilted his head so she would scratch his cheek and neck, and Maggie complied.

It had been a dreadful day. *Tomorrow will be better.* A hot bath and a good night's sleep, maybe a good book before that, would help tremendously. She held Snickers's blissful face between her hands, and he responded with a half purr, half meow.

"That's right. It's just you and me. And we're all right."

The phone rang and she sighed. Why did salespeople always have to call at dinnertime? She glanced at the partially eaten sandwich on the plate before her. Not that she was having much of a dinner.

She picked up Snickers, hauled him into the living room with her, and answered the phone.

"Hello?" she said in her I'm-not-buying-anything voice.

"Mom?"

"Emily." Maggie's mood immediately improved. "How are you?"

"I don't know. I feel so dumb."

Join the crowd, Maggie thought, but that probably wasn't the most helpful thing she could say. She put the cat on the floor and sat on the couch. "What's wrong, sweetheart? Didn't your tests go well?"

"I thought they did, especially psychology, but then after I got through with the last one—physiology—I started thinking about everything I should have included in my answers and what I could have done better, and now I'm sure I failed all three of them."

"Now, that can't be right, can it? You told me you were going to study some more."

"I did, Mom. I really did."

"Then why would you think you didn't pass?"

"I just think I could have done better. It's so much to remember, and I know I didn't remember everything while I was taking the test."

"Do you *know* that?" Maggie asked.

Emily was silent for a moment. "I guess I don't really *know* that. But I messed up one thing for sure. The question was about homeostasis, and I didn't know if it was Bernard or Cannon. I couldn't decide which one it was, and I checked in my book when I got back to the dorm, and I picked the wrong one."

Maggie had no idea what she was talking about. "That one mistake isn't going to fail you, is it?"

"No, not if that's all I missed, but I'm sure it's not. I only know that's one of them."

"I think you shouldn't worry about it, honey. Not at this point. It's over. Pass or fail, there's nothing you can do to change it."

Emily's voice was very small. "I know."

"And," Maggie said in her most no-nonsense voice, "you are *not* dumb. You know what's dumb? Getting taken in by a fake antique when antiques are supposed to be my business."

"What?"

"Yep. That pirate ring I gave that girl money for is a fake."

"Aw, Mom, why didn't you test it while she was there?"

"I did. And that one was real. But the one I have in my possession now is fake. So there's something strange going on for sure." Before Emily could say anything, Maggie cut her off. "And no, I haven't gone to the police about it yet."

"Mom."

"Not until I figure out a few things. I don't think any of this is exactly what meets the eye."

"I'd feel better if you'd let the experts handle it."

Maggie didn't say anything. She didn't know if she should admit the truth to her daughter or not. She let out an involuntary grunt.

"Mom," Emily pressed, "why not just tell the police?"

"Honey, I . . ." Maggie drew a deep breath, trying to keep the quaver out of her voice. "I don't want to ruin that girl's life. I keep thinking about how I would feel if you got mixed up in something bad and how I would want someone to try to help you out of it instead of turning you over to the police. Does that make sense?"

Emily laughed softly. "You're such a pushover. Did you ever think that maybe she doesn't want help? That she wants to keep taking advantage of people because it's easier than working for a living?"

"I don't know," Maggie admitted. "I don't know if it really is easier in the long run. But she's so young. Probably even younger than you."

"You make her sound like she's six, Mom."

"Well, she *is* young. You'd understand if you had seen her. She looked scared and desperate. I couldn't help thinking of you, especially since you're at school all by yourself."

"There are other people here, you know."

That made Maggie laugh. "I do. And I know you're going to be fine. And I'm going to be fine. We're both going to do what we need to do and not give up, right?"

"Right."

"Exactly. Now, I don't want you to worry about those exams. You've done all the work. You've done everything you can do. When are you supposed to get your grades?"

"Next week sometime."

"Okay then. Until 'next week sometime,' I want you to put it out of your mind and make an effort to do something fun. Or at least take it easy. Whatever you feel like doing. But as soon as you know how you did, will you call me?"

"Sure, Mom. The minute I hear."

"Good girl. Now you get a good night's sleep, and remember that worry gives you wrinkles."

"Ack!" Emily squawked. "You sound more like Grandma every day."

Maggie chuckled.

"Seriously, Mom, I want you to be careful. If there is something weird going on, I really wish you'd tell the police. I know you like figuring out little mysteries, but I'm afraid it's going to get you into real trouble someday."

"Oh, don't be silly. I don't do anything that's actually dangerous. Besides, what could possibly happen in a quaint little town like Somerset Harbor?"

"Seriously?"

"Okay. Don't answer that."

"Please, Mom. I really do worry about you."

"All right, I'll be careful. I promise. I might not ever hear from that girl again, you know. I could be stuck with a fake ring and another little mystery, one I'll never be able to solve."

"That would be fine with me."

"We'll see what happens. But don't worry. If it's anything serious, I'll talk to the police."

"Okay, Mom. Good night."

"Good night, sweetie. Call me soon, okay?"

"I will." Emily paused a second. "Love you, Mom."

"I love you too."

Maggie ended the call, put down the phone, and walked back toward the kitchen. Emily would be all right, Maggie was sure of that. And Maggie would be all right herself. Especially when she had Snickers—

"Snickers!"

When the big tabby's wide eyes met hers, Maggie saw that part of her peanut butter sandwich was missing. He took another bite and wolfed it down as fast as he could.

"Snickers, that's not yours!"

Snickers scanned his surroundings, clearly desperate for the nearest escape route. Before Maggie could reach him, he dove off the table with the rest of the sandwich hanging from his mouth and started for the stairs.

She blew out a frustrated breath and watched him run. Even the cat could dupe her, but at least his duping didn't feel so bad.

7

"It wasn't funny," Maggie protested the following morning at The Busy Bean.

James Bennett, Somerset Harbor's most eligible bachelor and respected town alderman, sat across from her. He leaned against the table, making it jiggle slightly as he made an obvious attempt to stifle his laughter.

"Oh yes it is." His blue eyes twinkled. "I can picture him stopping on the stairs, gobbling some of your sandwich until you were nearly within reach, and then dragging it up a few more steps every time you got too close."

She glared at him for a moment and then chuckled. "Okay, you're right. It was pretty funny. Especially when he got to the top of the stairs and tried to run into the front bedroom, then realized that the door was closed. He had no choice but to drop the sandwich and flee."

He wiped the corner of one eye, which now positively glistened with mirth. "I don't know how you ever catch him in that big house."

"I don't," she said. "I can't, and he knows it." With a rueful shake of her head, she picked up her coffee cup and took a sip. It was delicious as always. The Busy Bean café was filled with warmth and chatter. And it felt good to laugh.

"He's always entertaining," James said.

"He is. I don't know how much of it he actually ate. There was a small piece left when I finally caught up to him, and he'd left a few pieces on the stairs."

"I suppose he lay low the rest of the evening."

She shook her head and smirked. "Are you kidding? By the time I had everything cleaned up, he was following me around yowling because he could see the bottom of his food bowl. The cat knows no shame."

James took a bite of the cinnamon roll he'd ordered with his coffee. "Sounds like he keeps you on your toes."

"As if I needed something else."

His expression turned more serious. "Are you worried about Emily?"

"No." She stopped and then gave him a wry grin. "Well, no more than usual. I've made some less-than-stellar decisions at the shop recently, and I'm not quite sure if I'm going about fixing them the right way."

She told him briefly about Gail Lee, about the ring, and about what Pop Welborn had found out when he came to examine it.

"I suppose you want me to go to the police about it too," she said a little sulkily when it was all told.

"I think it would be a good idea," he said gently. "But I understand why you don't want to. I hope you're right about this girl. What did you say her name was?"

"Gail Lee. I suppose you don't know any Lees around here either."

One side of his mouth turned up. "Sorry."

"What about the notorious Solomon Zane? Do you know anything about him?"

The twinkle came back into his eyes. "Every boy loves pirate stories, right?"

"So what do you know?"

"Just the usual things. He terrorized the coast for twenty or thirty years until one day he disappeared without a trace. One of the townsmen and his sons supposedly hunted him down, but whether he actually killed Zane or not, nobody knows."

"Mrs. Ravenhurst says they did," Maggie said.

James chuckled. "She certainly does."

"I met her the other day. She came to talk to June about some pieces she wants for her house. Do you know her?"

"Not well, though I'm arranging the renovations for her home."

"Oh, that's great! You can tell me all about her."

He shrugged. "I don't know about *all*, but I can tell you some. Her house is off Sappington Drive, outside of town. Have you been out that way?"

"Not much," Maggie admitted. "I've heard there are some very nice homes there."

"Hers is a big Georgian. Two stories. Built in 1722 by Evander Ravenhurst. We're doing some restoration work, trying to preserve the foundation and stonework in one of the wings and pretty much shore up the whole house. We want to keep it structurally sound without spoiling the character of the place."

Maggie wrinkled her forehead. "Is it in bad shape?"

"Not very bad," James assured her. "But there's always going to be deterioration in a house that age. And she's let some of it go too long."

"That surprises me. I thought she'd be very concerned about the house since she's so involved with her family history."

James frowned. "From what I can tell, she expected Jake to take care of everything."

"Jake?"

"Jake Cobb. He's supposed to be the gardener and handyman and whatever else Mrs. Ravenhurst needs. Of course there are several other people who work for her, but Jake's the one she deals with directly, and he bosses the others. I think she hoped Hugh could be the boss, but he isn't quite up to it."

"Who's Hugh?"

"Hugh Green. His mother, Doris, has been the cook out at

the Ravenhurst place for as long as I can remember. Hugh tries hard, but it's more than he can handle. Jake bosses the people who work outside. Doris sees to anyone working inside, the maid and the cleaning woman and all that. If Mrs. Ravenhurst wants something done, she asks either of them, and they see that it's taken care of. She evidently didn't notice some of the things that need seeing to until recently, but Jake should have been aware of it."

Maggie chuckled. "I take it you don't care much for Mr. Cobb."

"I can't honestly say I do," James admitted. "He tries too hard to be likable, you know? Hugh and his mother are very loyal to Mrs. Ravenhurst, I'll give them that, but Jake . . . well, Jake's a little too clever for his own good, trying to worm his way into Mrs. Ravenhurst's good graces, hoping she'll take care of him in her will like she has the Greens. I wouldn't worry about that if he wasn't the smarmy type and a little bit of a bully on top of everything else."

"Charming," Maggie said.

"But I don't have much to do with him. Now that she realizes the extent of the work that needs to be done, Mrs. Ravenhurst is overseeing everything herself. I report directly to her, and she wants everything to be as authentic as possible."

"Yes, I got that impression when I met her earlier. I'm sure it will be lovely when it's all done. It's good to know she and June get along so well. I have a feeling she can be very hard to please."

James gazed up at the ceiling, whistling tunelessly.

"I'll take that as confirmation," Maggie said with a grin.

"You never heard it from me."

"What? What did I miss?" Daisy came over to the table, coffeepot in hand. "Y'all want a warm-up?"

"Yes, please." Maggie pushed her nearly empty cup toward the edge of the table, and Daisy filled it.

"How about you?" Daisy asked James.

"Just about half, thank you."

Daisy obliged and then gave him a knowing grin. "You two have been talking about that ring Maggie has, haven't you? And about Mrs. Ravenhurst. Did you find out something juicy about her family?"

James glanced at Maggie and then crooked his index finger at Daisy. She leaned closer.

"Can you keep a secret?" he asked, his voice low.

Daisy nodded, her big hair bouncing slightly.

"Good," he said. "So can I."

She put her free hand on her hip. "James Bennett, I ought to tell your mama on you."

He gave her a wink. "You do that, Daisy. She'd love to see you."

"I do need to pay her a call," she mused, and then she pursed her lips. "If only to tell her you need a good whooping."

"She already knows that."

Daisy laughed. "If you see her before I do, you make sure to tell her I said so."

"Yes ma'am."

"Oh, and tell her I saw her new quilt hanging up at The Quilt Cupboard." Daisy turned to Maggie. "Have you seen it?"

"The one with the embroidered leaves?" Maggie asked. "I saw it last month. It's lovely."

"No, the one with the appliquéd birds and vines and flowers. It's amazing." Daisy shook her head. "I don't know how she gets those stitches so small."

"Years of practice, I'd guess," Maggie remarked, turning to James for confirmation.

He nodded. "I can hardly remember ever seeing her sit down without some kind of handwork to do. She'll be pleased to hear you like it."

"All right. Well, I'll leave you two to your private talk. You let me know if there's anything you need." She gave James a humorously arch look. "Besides a whooping."

She sauntered off, hips swaying, and James took another drink of his coffee.

"You were telling me about Mrs. Ravenhurst," Maggie prompted.

"I don't know all that much. She had one son, I understand. He passed away several years ago. He had a couple of girls, but they've married and moved away. Neither of them decided to keep the Ravenhurst name." James raised one dark brow. "That's probably why they don't live in Somerset Harbor."

"Do you really think it's because of that?"

"I don't positively know, of course, but that's what people said when the girls' father died. Mrs. Ravenhurst was going to settle her whole estate on the two of them equally, provided they kept the Ravenhurst name and passed it on to their children. Evidently neither of them did. I doubt that was the only issue between them and their grandmother, but it seems to have been the last straw. I don't think either of the girls has been back to Maine in nearly ten years."

"That's sad." Maggie couldn't imagine losing her own daughter over something as trivial as the family name.

"Especially since she practically raised the girls in the first place. Their father, Paul, never actually left home. He brought his wife to the Ravenhurst mansion to live when he married, and the girls were brought up there, all of them dependent on Mrs. Ravenhurst. It was a little bit of a joke around town that Paul wouldn't buy a new pair of shoes without asking his mother's opinion."

"I guess that explains why the girls were ready to get out of Maine as soon as they could. It's too bad they couldn't be independent without having to break ties entirely."

"Yeah, it is." James shook his head. "They must be in their early thirties by now. Probably have kids of their own. It's a shame Mrs. Ravenhurst is missing out on them. I guess having the house and the name is all she needs."

"Sad," Maggie said again, promising herself she would never make Emily feel so suffocated that she felt she had to run away. "She does have her housekeeper, I suppose, but she doesn't really seem the type to sit down to a cup of tea with an employee, does she?"

James laughed softly. "Not really. She is on several boards of directors though. And some of the local charities, the historical preservation guild, one of the genealogical societies, I think. She stays busy at any rate."

Maggie picked up her cup, not drinking, but enjoying the heat of the coffee through the porcelain. "She seems the type who'd be interested in the historical society. I'm surprised she's not a member. Maybe next time she's in the shop, I'll ask her if she'd like to start coming to our meetings."

"Not if you want to stay a member yourself."

Maggie frowned. "What do you mean?"

"My understanding is that back in the day, Mrs. Ravenhurst *was* the historical society. She pretty much ran things and the other ladies did things her way. But when the old guard started dying off, some of the younger ones didn't want to play her game. There were evidently some epic battles—exquisitely polite, of course—but when the smoke cleared, Mrs. Ravenhurst found herself on the outside looking in."

Maggie gaped at him. "They asked her to leave?"

"Not that I ever heard," James said. "It was more along the lines that they would either play her way or she would take her toys and go home. They almost lost the house the society meets in because Mrs. Ravenhurst withdrew her financial support, and they had a hard time scraping together the money for taxes and upkeep and all that sort of thing. But everybody pulled together, and they made it work."

"I bet that made things interesting."

"I suppose that's why she doesn't come into town very often." James appeared thoughtful for a moment. "And when she does, she's very businesslike about it."

Maggie thought back to when Mrs. Ravenhurst was in the shop, very businesslike and as regal and distant as a queen. *And as lonely.*

"Then I suppose an invitation to the next meeting of the historical society is out," Maggie said. "Still, there has to be a way to make friends with her."

James leaned across the table toward Maggie, his eyes warm. "You've got a good heart, Maggie."

Maggie felt a touch of heat in her face. "Everybody should have friends, right?" She fumbled with her coffee cup.

"You're not from here," he said thoughtfully, "so you and she wouldn't have a lot of baggage from the past, but you have ties to Somerset Harbor, so you're not a total outsider. And she and your aunt got along pretty well." Finally, he nodded. "Maybe you're the kind of friend Mrs. Ravenhurst needs."

"I'm going to give it a try," Maggie said. "If she'll let me."

8

Whenever she had time the next morning, Maggie studied the information Pop Welborn had given her and the copies she had made from the historical society. She borrowed the book and the notebook Ruth had at the historical society, trying to see if there was something in either that she had missed, but there wasn't anything that Ruth hadn't shown her earlier.

Though she knew the name of the pirate and his ship, she found precious little about him on the Internet. He was mostly a brief mention in articles about piracy in general, though some contemporary newspaper accounts indicated he had a fearsome reputation up and down the coast. His disappearance was seen as nothing less than the doing of a just and merciful Providence, as she'd read in the article she'd originally found.

"Are you still trying to track down that pirate?" June asked. "I'd have given up by now."

Maggie glanced up from the computer screen. "You haven't given up on finding those mint-condition Queen Anne armchairs for Mrs. Ravenhurst."

"Those armchairs mean income," June reminded her gently.

"True. How can I help?"

June slapped a notepad down next to the keyboard. "I made a list of all the places that might have what we're looking for, including some places that specialize in estate sales. It would be great if you could call them up and tell them what we need. Most of them are going to say they have exactly what we want, and most of them will be wrong. But if they claim to have something, ask them to e-mail a photo or a link so we can give it a look."

Maggie called every number on the list and, after nearly two hours on the phone, ended up with four likely candidates.

"These might do," she said, handing June a piece of paper that was now covered with notes, check marks, and crossed-out names. "They're going to send me pictures. Mrs. Ravenhurst should be pleased."

"Mrs. Ravenhurst will be pleased when we find her the right chairs and not before."

Maggie chuckled. "I've heard she can be a trial."

"She's . . . interesting, to say the least. I've never heard her raise her voice or say anything that wasn't absolutely polite, but somehow she can make you feel like an absolute idiot if you disappoint her."

Maggie frowned at June speculatively. "You must have heard her story about how her Lacey ancestor vanquished the notorious pirate in defense of his daughter's honor. What does Mrs. Ravenhurst say happened?"

"Zane kidnapped her 'X number of greats' great-grandmother from the Lacey lineage out of her bed one night, and her father and brothers rescued her and dispatched Zane without mercy. They were the only ones brave enough to stop the pirate and bring order and decency to Somerset Harbor. And when her Ravenhurst ancestor came to town and married the girl who had been rescued, his successful commercial ventures brought prosperity and stability to the whole region. And of course, both parties were the bluest of blue bloods. Mrs. Ravenhurst makes sure to emphasize that in her story."

"I don't think Pop agrees with the way she tells it. Not about the blue blood, of course, but about what the girl's father and brothers did and what happened to Zane himself."

"Really?" June sat on the edge of the counter. "I didn't know there was any dispute about that."

"Pop thinks the father would have been too old and out of shape to take on a cutthroat like Zane, and his boys would have been too young. They were barely in their teens at the time."

June raised both eyebrows. "Then what happened to Zane?"

"Well, Pop doesn't rule out that it happened the way Mrs. Ravenhurst says, but he doesn't think it's very likely. He thinks it's more probable that his first mate might have gotten rid of him so he could take the ship, but it's just as likely that the old rogue died of a tropical fever, or food poisoning, or pretty much anything else."

June frowned. "Then how'd the girl get away? He wouldn't have simply let her go. Not without the ransom being paid."

"Pop doesn't know about that. He gave me copies of some information he had, some contemporary newspaper articles and that sort of thing. There's not much, but he thinks some of it might have been hushed up so the girl's family didn't have to deal with the scandal anymore. What's there is pretty fuzzy."

"What did it say?"

"The girl was kidnapped and Zane demanded ransom," Maggie said. "Before her father could get the money together, she showed up on the beach, alone and unharmed."

"That's pretty amazing. What did she say about it?"

"According to the newspaper account, she was so distraught over her experience that she didn't recall anything. She remembered going to sleep in her bed the night she was taken and then seeing her father coming toward her on the beach. The doctor who attended her made some remarks about delicate female sensibilities, and evidently that was sufficient."

June snorted. "Hmmm. And the girl was all right after that?"

"It seems like it. I don't suppose the original Mr. Ravenhurst would have married her if she had been damaged in any way."

"Did you find out anything about him?" June asked. "I don't think I ever heard much about him except that he was a wealthy businessman."

"That's about all I know too," Maggie admitted. "But I'm not sure what that has to do with Zane."

"Maybe Ravenhurst was the one who dispatched Zane, not the girl's father."

Maggie shrugged. "I don't know how that could be. He didn't meet Miss Lacey until a year or more after the kidnapping. Zane was long gone by then." She thought for a moment. "I wonder, since he was new to Somerset Harbor, if he didn't know about the incident until after he married the girl."

"I'm sure there's some information about them on the Internet, in the library, or in the historical society archives."

"Right. It won't help me figure out what happened to my pirate, but I'd like to know what happened to the Ravenhursts besides that they built the Ravenhurst mansion and lived there for the rest of their lives. I guess I could do a quick search and see what I can find." Before she started the search, Maggie checked the shop e-mail. "Oh, look. We already have a couple of responses about the chairs."

. . . .

That evening, Maggie sat at her own computer, trying to find out more about the Ravenhurst who had come to Somerset Harbor, married the daughter of the town's wealthiest merchant, and built the Ravenhurst mansion. She hoped she would have better luck than she and June had had earlier. One of the places that had responded to her request for matching Queen Anne chairs in mint condition had e-mailed her photographs of two chairs that didn't match. One was actually Queen Anne, or at least a period replica, but it was so battered that it was a wonder it could even support its own weight, much less the weight of anyone who might wish to sit in it. The other chair looked almost Danish modern, but there were so many layers of yellow paint on it, it was hard to tell exactly what it was.

The other response was much more interesting. It was from an estate sale agent June had bought from in the past. The agent apologized for the quality of the photograph but said the chairs were a matched pair of authentic Queen Anne chairs in excellent condition, which had been in the same family since they were made in the 1720s. She said she would try to get a better picture of them and send it along when she could, but she also advised that she had another buyer who had expressed interest in the pair.

From what Maggie could tell, the chairs were upholstered in rich, dusky-rose damask and had lovely carved bellflower cabriole legs and hoof feet. If the chairs were genuine, they might be precisely what Mrs. Ravenhurst wanted. Of course they might need reupholstering or other restoration work, but Maggie and June were used to that. If Maggie was going to have a chance at them, she'd have to make an offer quickly.

But she'd deal with that tomorrow. If she didn't receive a better photo, she'd probably have to go out and see the chairs herself. The agent had a shop about twenty miles from Somerset Harbor. If the chairs were right for the Ravenhurst home, it would definitely be worth the drive. She wanted Mrs. Ravenhurst to be pleased with whatever she bought. And maybe that would be the beginning of a friendship between her and Maggie. *It's possible, right?*

Maybe if Maggie knew more about the original Mr. Ravenhurst, it would give her something to talk about with Mrs. Ravenhurst. The woman was obviously proud of her ancestry, and it would be fun to find out the little details that would have been passed down through the family and weren't recorded in history books or newspapers. But Maggie had to start somewhere.

She rubbed Snickers's head as he lay sprawled out next to her keyboard. "Good thing we have the Internet, huh, boy?"

He purred in response, which she took as assent.

"All right then, from the top."

She typed in *Ravenhurst, Somerset Harbor, Maine,* but all that got her was page after page of links to Willa Ravenhurst's charitable endeavors. Maggie glanced briefly at the obituary for her son, Paul David Ravenhurst, who had passed away thirteen years before, when he was only forty-four years old.

"That's a shame," she told Snickers, whose tail flopped once against the table. "He was my age. Poor Mrs. Ravenhurst."

She scanned the next two pages of search results, but neither of them was what she wanted. Finally she added *1722* to her search. That brought up a few new links.

"This one looks good."

The Ravenhurst mansion had been featured in a magazine on historic homes four years ago, and the article was still in the publication's blog archives. Maggie clicked on the link, which brought up slick color photos of a large Georgian mansion painted white with forest-green trim. There were pictures of the inside as well. A large stone fireplace, a gorgeous cherrywood bombé chest, a claw-foot tub, and a cast-iron stove were just some of the period treasures in Mrs. Ravenhurst's house. It would be wonderful to visit in person, to see all the little knickknacks and historical furniture the Ravenhursts, past and present, had collected over nearly three hundred years. Maggie read the article.

Right outside Somerset Harbor on the Maine coast is the Ravenhurst mansion. Built in 1722 by wealthy London merchant Evander Ravenhurst for his young bride, Caroline Lacey, it features all the characteristics of classic Georgian architecture with its highly symmetrical design, multipaned windows evenly balanced on either side of a central front door, chimneys at either end of the home, gabled dormers, and a two-story portico. Inside the spacious entrance hall there is a graciously curved stairway that leads to generously proportioned parlors and bedrooms.

The article described more of the structure and furnishings. Toward the end, it mentioned Mrs. Ravenhurst and stated that there had always been a Ravenhurst living in the mansion since its construction. It included a photograph of Mrs. Ravenhurst, coolly regal as she perched on a settee before one of the windows at the front of the house, her linen suit of pale gold a perfect match to her surroundings. Other than that, there was nothing more about the Ravenhursts themselves.

"I still don't know much about the first Mr. Ravenhurst and his wife," Maggie told Snickers. She found that he was sound asleep and snoring softly. "Fine help you are."

She typed the name *Evander Ravenhurst* into her search engine and was rewarded with a list of links. She found a few references to his business dealings in lumber and shipbuilding and noted that he had served as a judge in the Somerset Harbor area from 1735 until his death in 1762. He and his wife had three sons and one daughter, and from all accounts, lived productive, charitable, and contented lives, in general leaving the world a better place for having been in it.

There was nothing about what the couple looked like, but she suspected Mrs. Ravenhurst had their portraits prominently displayed in her home. She did, however, find a photograph of their tombstones on one of the genealogy sites.

Evander's read:

> *EVANDER RAVENHURST*
> *Judge and Merchant, lyeth here interred*
> *Born April 17, 1693*
> *Died in Jesus, December 31, 1762*
> *Aged 69 years*
> *Flown to that place of Reunion*
> *and no more Mourning,*
> *a Memorie departed.*

> *Therefore, if any man be in Christ, he is a new creature: old things are passed away; behold, all things are become new.*

> *2 Corinthians 5:17*

Caroline's was engraved:

> *Here lyeth ye body of*
> *CAROLINE LACEY RAVENHURST*
> *devoted wife of Evander Ravenhurst, Judge of this towne*
> *Born July 9, 1700*
> *Died in Jesus, October 2, 1762*
> *Aged 62 years*
> *Forever mourned.*

> *Who can find a virtuous woman? for her price is far above rubies. The heart of her husband doth safely trust in her, so that he shall have no need of spoil. She will do him good and not evil all the days of her life.*

> *Proverbs 31:10-12*

There was something beautiful and heartbreaking about the words. Clearly, Evander Ravenhurst had loved his wife and had been unable to go on very long without her. It was an unexpectedly romantic thing to find on a tombstone but a comforting one as well. They had their faith and even in death were not without hope. The image of Richard's tombstone flashed into her mind: *Beloved husband and father.* Somehow it didn't seem like enough.

She blinked hard and then shook her head. Even after this long, even when she was happy and enjoying her life in Maine, there were still moments when her memories crept up on her and exposed a hidden pocket of grief she hadn't known was there. But she knew this was normal, all part of the healing process. It would pass. She would go on. Richard would have expected nothing less.

She noticed Snickers was awake again, watching her with narrowed green eyes, so she stroked his head. "Maybe we'd better get back to the pirate. There's nothing very exciting or scandalous about Mr. and Mrs. Ravenhurst." She sighed wistfully. "But I bet I would have liked them."

She investigated the genealogy site a little more thoroughly and found a rather extensive listing of Evander Ravenhurst's descendants. Working her way through the line of his oldest son, John, she eventually found Willa Ravenhurst; her son, Paul David Ravenhurst; and his two daughters, Amanda Littlefield and Rachel Cortez. Amanda's son, Aiden, had been born about seven years before. For now, that was all there was.

For all practical purposes, the Ravenhurst line, at least that branch of it, had ended with Mrs. Ravenhurst's son. Or more properly, with her quarrel with her granddaughters. Maggie thought back to a song her grandfather used to sing about a loveless mansion on a hill. She didn't know who had originally sung the song or any of the other words to it, but those were enough. What would Evander Ravenhurst think now of that mansion he had built for his beloved bride nearly three hundred years ago?

"This is not going to help me figure out what happened to the real pirate or the real pirate ring," Maggie scolded herself. "And I can't wave a magic wand and make Mrs. Ravenhurst mend fences with her granddaughters. Her priorities are none of my business, are they, boy?"

Snickers made a squawking meow and, with a stretch, hopped off the desk and trotted toward the kitchen.

Maggie glanced at her watch. "Ah. I see it's past dinnertime."

She followed the cat to the pantry. She'd done enough investigating for one day, but that didn't mean she was hanging up her magnifying glass and deerstalker. She'd talk to Mrs. Ravenhurst herself the first chance she got. Surely the woman knew some old family stories that would hold at least a few clues to the fate of the notorious Solomon Zane . . . if she were willing to share them.

9

The next day dawned blustery and rainy, and Maggie wanted nothing more than to stay curled up in bed with Snickers and read her favorite Agatha Christie, *And Then There Were None*. But the shop didn't close simply because it was miserable outside, so she forced herself out of the warm covers and into a hot shower.

At the shop, June was her usual perky self, already on the telephone to some of her sources, trying to track down an armoire that would complement the rest of the furniture in Mrs. Ravenhurst's bedroom.

"Did you ever get a better picture of those chairs?" June asked when she hung up the phone.

Maggie shook her head. "I plan to give the woman a call and see if they're still available. What else do we have going on today?"

"Mrs. Adams is interested in the Sheraton sideboard, but she doesn't want to pay what it's worth. How much do you want me to come down on it?"

Maggie frowned. Mrs. Adams had haggled the price the last time she bought something. "Let me think about it. What else?"

"The couple from Portland wants to know if they can return the Hepplewhite dining set and get the Chippendale instead."

"If they want to pay the difference, that's fine. We haven't delivered the Hepplewhite yet, right?"

"It was supposed to go today, but I took it off the list."

"Good." Maggie gazed around the shop. "And we've got to find something to put in the front window where that inlaid end table was. It looks bare without it."

They spent the morning seeing to everything that needed to be done. It was lunchtime before either of them had a chance to take a break.

Maggie stretched her arms over her head. "I'm starved. What do you think? Do we dare close up for an hour and go over to The Busy Bean?"

June seemed tempted, then looked unsure. "I don't know. I brought my lunch, and I really should get the end-of-the-month accounting done. Carol Clarke is coming in at two, and I still have to figure out what a good price would be for that Spanish chest she's interested in. It's a fascinating piece, but part of the trim is really damaged, and not in a 'gives it character' sort of way. I really shouldn't go—"

"Sure you should." Maggie grinned. "Come on. I'll buy."

"I don't know. If the boss finds out . . ."

Maggie took her arm and turned her toward the door. "If the boss finds out, I'll tell her the owner said it was fine. Come on. The sun's finally out. We don't want to be stuck in here all day."

June put down her clipboard and picked up her keys. "I'll put a note on the door saying we'll be back in an hour."

. . . .

Maggie breathed in the brisk, rain-scented air as she and June strode down Shoreline Drive to The Busy Bean. The sun had indeed made an appearance, turning everything a soft watercolor gold. She told June about what she had found about the Ravenhursts the night before.

"Unfortunately, none of that has anything to do with Solomon Zane or his disappearance," she concluded as they walked up to the door.

"I'd be more concerned about the disappearance of your ring," June said.

Maggie stepped into The Busy Bean and inhaled deeply. "Right now, all I'm thinking about is contributing to the disappearance of some of Daisy's yummy-smelling coffee."

She was disappointed to see that her favorite table by the window was occupied, but she didn't have a chance to do more than scan the room for an empty place before the couple seated there got up.

"I'll have this ready for you in a jiffy, Maggie." Jenny, a young waitress, hurried over to the table, whisked the dirty plates onto a tray, and then wiped down the table. "There you go. Have a seat and I'll get you some silverware. Coffee for both of you?"

Maggie nodded and thanked her, and then she and June sat down. "It's so nice to go someplace where people know you."

"Everybody knows everybody in this town," June said.

"Except nobody knows Gail Lee. I've about run out of people to ask about her."

June thought for a minute. "Did you try the post office?"

"Do you think someone there would know her?"

"There's probably a picture of her posted on the wall."

Maggie tried to look stern but ended up laughing instead. "That's bad. Even if she is a thief, I doubt she's one of the FBI's most wanted. I sure would like to have a talk with her." She glanced around the room, and then her eyes narrowed as she spotted a man drinking coffee at the end of the counter. "I wish there was some way I could pin it on him."

June followed her gaze, then turned back to Maggie and made a face. "That Edmund Peters. He always looks like he's up to something."

Maggie groaned under her breath. "He's spotted us and is coming over here."

Peters sauntered over to their table, coffee cup in hand.

"Ladies." He smiled, displaying plentiful teeth. "I was going to come by your shop after lunch, Mrs. Watson."

"Were you?" Maggie asked as pleasantly as she could manage.

"I was going to see if we could come to some agreement on that very interesting ring with the sea serpent on it. You haven't sold it yet, have you?"

"It hasn't been sold, no," Maggie said, watching his eyes. "Your offer was $1,500, I believe."

"Fifteen hundred. After I have it authenticated, of course."

Maggie was surprised. "You know it's a nineteenth-century replica, right?"

His heavy brows disappeared into his lank hair. "Replica? Oh no. The ring I saw the other day was the genuine article. I'd swear to it."

Maggie glanced at June. That was an odd way of putting it, unless he knew about the substitution.

"It was," Maggie told him. "But now it's not. Someone switched it for a fake. After you looked at it." Her smile was mildly challenging.

He didn't even flinch. "It's a good thing I didn't buy it then, isn't it."

The smug little worm, he knows something about what happened to the real ring. But what? "You don't happen to know a girl named Gail Lee, do you?" Maggie asked, and this time his bafflement seemed genuine.

"Gail Lee? No."

"In her teens. Slim. Dishwater blonde."

"I don't know anyone like that," Peters said. "Why?"

"She's the one who sold me the ring originally. It was genuine then."

He snorted. "Oldest trick in the book. Sell the real thing and then have someone else come switch it for a fake." He sneered at June. "I don't know how you all stay in business if you don't take better care of your merchandise than that."

June's mouth tightened. "Funny that you were the only one who had a chance to steal it."

"Me?" Peters protested, his pasty skin reddening. "What, with her watching me every second?"

"Except when Mrs. Ravenhurst came in," Maggie reminded him.

"And I just happened to have an exact replica in my pocket in case there was an opportunity? Right," Peters scoffed, and then he leaned a bit closer to Maggie. "I wouldn't be surprised if it wasn't the old bat herself who took that ring. If there was a copy of Solomon Zane's ring among the family heirlooms, she'd be the one who had it."

Maggie narrowed her eyes at him. "How do you know it was Zane's ring?"

"You forget, Mrs. Watson, I've been in the history business for a long time. I knew that was Zane's ring when I got the e-mail about it in the first place."

That was true. Or at least he had claimed to know something about it at the time.

"You mark my words," he said. "That copy was in Mrs. Ravenhurst's family all along. It was probably one of them who had it made. She could easily have switched it out."

"Don't be ridiculous," June said. "She wasn't anywhere near the ring."

Maggie thought for a moment. Had she been? Mrs. Ravenhurst had to have at least walked close to the counter where Peters had been standing when she came into the shop to talk to June. It was impossible to get into the storage area without going past it.

"I don't think it could have been her," Maggie said. "You were standing right by the ring when she came in. You'd have seen."

"Maybe," he said. "Who's to say she didn't hire someone to make the swap later on? Once she'd seen the real thing was there."

Maggie didn't have an answer for that. Evidently, neither did June.

Peters smirked at them, obviously feeling he had won his point. "Now I can't say I wouldn't like to have that copy. If it's really a nineteenth-century replica, it would go nicely in my collection." There was a hint of sliminess now in his smile. "What do you say?"

"I'm sorry," Jenny said, hurrying back with two steaming cups of coffee and a handful of silverware. "Things are a little busy right now." She edged around Peters and set it all out on the table for Maggie and June. "Are you ready to order?"

"Yes," Maggie said.

"Ladies," Peters said with a stiff nod. Then he stalked back to the counter where the remains of his lunch awaited him.

They both ordered club sandwiches and apple pie. When Jenny left to turn in their order, Maggie glanced toward the lunch counter where Peters had been sitting. He was gone.

"The little pest," June said, stirring sugar and cream into her coffee. "I wouldn't be at all surprised if he didn't have your ring in the first place."

"I still don't think that would make sense. He'd have to have been in on it with the girl, if that were the case, and if they already had the genuine ring, why sell it to me in the first place? And for a measly $500? He'd know it was worth more than that if he knew the history, and he would have given her a number to hold out for."

"I guess that doesn't seem very likely, does it?" June admitted. "But it seems less likely that Mrs. Ravenhurst took it. I mean, Mrs. Ravenhurst? *Really?*"

Maggie chuckled. "You know her much better than I do, but that does seem a little far-fetched. I suppose she could have seen it when she was in the shop, but if she wanted it so badly, wouldn't she just buy it?"

"Yeah, she probably would. As proud as her family has always been of their pirate-vanquishing history, you'd think she'd want to buy it and display it prominently. I guess it does make sense that if her family got the original ring from Zane himself at the time of his death, someone along the line would have had a copy made so he could wear it around town without risking the original."

"That's what Pop Welborn said the copy was probably made for." Maggie took a drink of coffee, thinking. "But if the Ravenhursts had the genuine ring in the first place, how did Gail Lee get it?"

"Anything could have happened to the original over the past three hundred years," June said. "You won't believe the stories behind some of the things we get in at the shop. It could have been lost or stolen or put up on a losing wager. It could have been inherited by someone who left the Ravenhurst house, maybe by a relative who married and moved away, or a grandson or great-grandson who never lived there. Anything could have happened to it. Maybe Mrs. Ravenhurst doesn't even know it exists."

"That's certainly possible," Maggie said, knowing the task of tracking down the ring and the fate of its original owner had now gotten exponentially more difficult. "And it's possible the Ravenhursts never had the ring at all. It could have been passed down to someone in Zane's family."

"Two club sandwiches," Daisy announced, appearing next to their table, her perky smile crinkling the corners of her eyes. "And I brought y'all some of our sweet-potato chips because they're your favorite, Miss Maggie. On the house."

"Oh, hi, Daisy," Maggie said. "Thank you."

"We were getting busy, so I asked Jenny to come in. Actually, we've been swamped since about ten."

"Miss?" a man called from two tables over.

"Sorry, got to go. You two enjoy your lunch." Daisy hurried away.

Maggie popped a sweet-potato chip into her mouth. "Delicious."

June shuddered. "I don't care for any, thanks. You go ahead."

Maggie chuckled and snatched another one. "More for me."

"You're welcome to them," June said, making a face. "Anyway, back to the ring being passed down to someone in Zane's family. Did he have any family? I thought his only son died a year or so after he disappeared. Whenever Zane's ship and crew were finally taken."

"True." Maggie groaned. "Don't make it harder than it already is. The ring could have been taken by anybody from the Ravenhursts down to the hangman who executed Zane's first mate, and after that, it could have gone anywhere."

"But that brings us back to one question," June reminded her. "Where did Gail Lee get it?"

"And we won't know that until we figure out who and where she is." Maggie took a huge bite of her sandwich and chewed aggressively. "But she can't hide forever."

"Slow down. What did that sandwich ever do to you?" June said in mock alarm.

"Sorry," Maggie said, "but this is so frustrating."

"Anything I can help with?" a deep male voice asked.

Maggie and June looked up to see James standing next to their table, coffee cup in hand and a mischievous glint in his blue eyes. "Or am I interrupting a secret business meeting?"

Maggie patted the chair beside her. "Have a seat. I'm still

trying to find out about this mysterious ring I have on my hands. You haven't found out anything about this Gail Lee, have you?"

He sat down with a regretful shake of his head. "Not a trace, I'm afraid. I even asked my mother if she knew of anyone like that. Or if she knew of any Lees in Somerset Harbor or anywhere else."

"And?"

"She knew a family called Lee back in the '60s, but they moved off a long time ago. She thinks it's pretty unlikely this girl has anything to do with them."

"Another dead end." Maggie poked at her chips. "And I haven't come up with any more information about the ring either. Maybe I should ask Mrs. Ravenhurst about it next time she's in the shop."

"She's supposed to come in at one thirty." June picked up the last bite of her sandwich. "I'm going to show her that new end table we got and then—"

"It's twenty after," James said.

June's eyes widened as she glanced at the beehive clock on the wall. "Yikes! I'd better get going. Mrs. Ravenhurst won't be very happy if she gets there and the door's locked." She stood up and put her wadded-up napkin on the table. "Your treat, right?"

Maggie nodded. "Right. Go on back. I'll meet you there."

"Thanks. Sorry to eat and run." June waved at James and hurried away.

"You don't want to keep Mrs. Ravenhurst waiting," James said. "Ask me how I know."

Maggie grinned. "At least you lived to tell the tale."

"She's not so bad," he admitted. "But she does have very explicit expectations."

"I wish I could sit down and talk with her. Get to know her better. Listen to her stories. She's always very businesslike at the shop." Maggie gazed at him for a moment, a little smile coming to her lips. "She must be much more relaxed at her own home."

He suddenly looked wary. "What are you up to now?"

"Nothing." The little smile turned coy. "How can you accuse me of being up to something?"

"Maggie," he said sternly.

"I only thought how nice it would be if I could possibly, maybe, come with you when you go to her house sometime to consult with her about her restoration."

He narrowed his eyes at her. "Because?"

"I thought we could have a little chat about her antiques and her lovely home and how Carriage House Antiques could work with you so everything is exactly right when it's all done. You know, to be neighborly."

"And you'll just happen to ask her to tell you her pirate story too, right?"

She shrugged. "It might come up. If that's what *she* wants to talk about, of course."

He chuckled. "I'm sure she'll be happy to tell it to you. And happy to show her home to someone who actually appreciates the history behind it. But remember I'll be there on business, and she's pretty no-nonsense when it comes to that. She might not have time to sit down and chat."

"I realize that. Honestly, James, I would like to get to know her. She seems so alone in that big house. I've probably already dug up everything that's in her pirate story anyway."

"True. And a lot of that is pretty likely to have been embellished by the family over the years."

"So I can come with you?"

"All right," he said, folding his arms and obviously trying not to grin. "But you'd better behave yourself."

She raised her right hand. "You have my word."

10

The next morning, Maggie rode with James out to the Ravenhurst mansion. The descriptions she had read about it and the photographs she had seen of it didn't do it justice. The eastern wing was surrounded by scaffolding and piles of board and brick, but that didn't detract from its grandeur. Except for the workmen's trucks, there was nothing in sight that would have been out of place in the 1720s.

"Beautiful," Maggie said as they walked up the front steps. "It's magnificent."

"Needs a little work," James said, admiration in his eyes as he looked the place over. "But I think it'll do."

His knock was answered by a short, heavyset woman likely in her sixties. Her iron-gray hair was pulled into a bun as severe as her expression.

"Mr. Bennett. Good morning." She eyed Maggie with suspicion. "Won't you both come in?"

Maggie ventured a hopeful smile. "Good morning. You must be Doris."

The other woman's mouth tightened, but before she could reply, James spoke up. "Maggie, *Mrs. Green* has been at the Ravenhurst home for over thirty years."

Maggie winced, realizing she had already gotten off on the wrong foot by calling the woman by her first name.

"Nearly forty," Mrs. Green said.

"You must have been very young when you came here, Mrs. Green." Maggie began to worry that her quite-forced smile was turning into a grimace.

"Just out of school, ma'am." Mrs. Green glanced questioningly at James as they walked into the long entrance hall.

"I beg your pardon," he said. "This is Ms. Watson, from the antiques shop Mrs. Ravenhurst has been working with. We thought it would be a good idea for her to come out and see the house and the work my crew is doing so she'll know a little better what Mrs. Ravenhurst wants."

Maggie tried the smile again. "Please call me Maggie."

The housekeeper's stoic expression did not change. "Come this way, ma'am."

Mrs. Green marched ahead of them. Maggie wanted very much to stop and admire the lovely antiques they passed, including the gorgeous cherrywood bombé chest she had seen in the Internet article, but she didn't dare slow down until they reached what must have been the formal sitting room. It looked much as it had in the article, all white and pale gold, everything in the room suited to the period and perfectly coordinated. The lady of the house sat on the brocade settee in front of the windows, wearing a blouse of peach-colored silk, black slacks, and a wide belt. She might have been in her eighties, but she was still tall and trim and dressed in a style that not only flattered her but also made a subtle statement about her wealth and position.

"Mr. Bennett and Ms. Watson, ma'am," Mrs. Green announced.

Mrs. Ravenhurst seemed mildly surprised. "I didn't expect you to bring a guest, James. How are you, Maggie?"

Maggie went to her and shook her outstretched hand. "I hope you don't mind my coming along. James and I were talking, and I thought I could do a much better job finding the kinds of things you like if I could see the space and what you have already. I read the magazine article they did on your home a few years ago, but there's so much more I haven't seen."

"Did you?" Mrs. Ravenhurst looked pleasantly surprised.

"I'd quite forgotten about that article. They were all over the house with their cameras and such, moving things around where they didn't belong. They very nearly smashed that piece over there." She pointed to a blue-and-white Delft serving platter on the picture rail by the window. "They had people with lights and cords and heaven knows what swarming through the house like cockroaches."

Maggie glanced at James, trying not to giggle. His expression told her that would be a mistake. She opted for commiseration instead.

"That must have been awful."

"Oh, not so bad, really. It was worth it to share the house with the world." Mrs. Ravenhurst lifted her chin, pursing her lips slightly. "There aren't many left like it. Not many that have been left almost exactly as they were built back in the early eighteenth century."

Maggie nodded eagerly. "That's another reason why I asked James to let me come with him today. I wanted to see your house for myself."

Mrs. Ravenhurst inclined her head slightly.

"It would be good for her to see what I'm doing too," James added. "That way she and I are more or less on the same page."

Mrs. Ravenhurst stood, a smug expression on her face. "Then you'd better let me show you around the place, Maggie. James, there are a few things I want to ask you about anyway, if you'd be good enough to come with us. I'll explain as we go along."

She took them all through the house, first through the downstairs, the stately dining room, the library Maggie could have spent a week exploring, the formal parlors and sitting rooms—all of it looking as if it belonged in the early eighteenth century. The modern appliances in the stone-floored kitchen were carefully concealed in wooden cupboards, and the blazing hearth with its pot hooks and roasting spit appeared to be the only means of cooking meals.

The upstairs decor was slightly more relaxed, but not much. Mrs. Ravenhurst had a small office in what seemed to have been a bedroom once. But there, too, apart from the large flat-screen monitor on the secretary desk, the computer and printer and other technology were concealed behind cabinet doors.

Mrs. Ravenhurst's bedroom was also more impressive than the photographs had depicted. The grand four-poster bed was hung with fine cream-colored linen, and the valance and coverlet were hand embroidered with leaves and flowers. The valances at the large windows had been made to match.

Maggie stopped to admire the needlework, and she managed to keep her hands to herself despite the almost overwhelming desire to touch it. "This is amazing."

"It's not antique," Mrs. Ravenhurst admitted. "But I did have it specially made. Of course, the style is Jacobean and not Queen Anne, but I thought it was so very pretty."

"I like it," Maggie told her. "It's as if your family in the 1720s had an antique coverlet and hangings of their own."

Mrs. Ravenhurst's smile finally looked genuine. "I always think of it precisely like that." She pointed out to James a place in the wall where the plaster was starting to crack, and then she gestured toward the corridor. "Come, let me show you the rest of the floor."

There was a cozy little parlor done in cream and blue and several more bedrooms, lovely and filled with light. At the end of the wing were two bedrooms that were adjoined by a sitting room.

"This is nice," Maggie said, peeping in when Mrs. Ravenhurst did not invite them inside. "I wonder if this wasn't once a suite for a married couple or a playroom between two children's rooms."

Mrs. Ravenhurst did not reply but threw open the door that led to the third floor. "Doris and Hugh have their rooms up here. There are a number of small bedrooms that once housed the staff when there was much more manual labor to be done. We mostly use them for storage now. There's really not much to see up here, except there are some leaks in the dormer windows I'd like you to see, James. And there's another crack in the wall in this room."

She opened one of the doors, revealing a little room stacked with boxes, some of them marked with an *A* and some with an *R*. Besides the crack in the wall, there was nothing more to see.

"I'll make sure this gets taken care of too," James said as he ran his hand over it. "And you'd better show me which windows you're talking about. You say the leaks are in the windows themselves, right? Not coming from the roof?"

"I don't believe so."

Still talking about the leak, the two of them walked across the corridor and into one of the rooms with a dormer window. Maggie stayed behind for a moment more, puzzling over the boxes. A *and* R? *What are the names of Mrs. Ravenhurst's grand-daughters?* Maggie couldn't remember. One of them might have been Amanda.

Oh, good heavens ... what had she said back there about the children's rooms with the adjoining playroom? Could that have been the granddaughters' rooms when they still lived here? There was no evidence in anything Maggie had seen so far that a child had ever lived in this house, though there must have been many over the past three hundred years. Had Mrs. Ravenhurst packed up every trace of those girls once their father had died and she realized she could no longer preside over their lives?

Maggie put her hand on one of the boxes, tempted but not daring to open it and see what was inside. Mrs. Ravenhurst had kept it. Whatever was in there that had once belonged to the girls, she had kept it. How sad that was, and how lonely the woman must be. *But proud.* Too proud to ask for forgiveness and reconciliation.

"Maggie?" James stuck his head in the door. "Did you get lost?"

"Lost in thought," she said, hurrying out into the hallway. "What did I miss?"

"Not much. A couple of leaky windowpanes. I don't see any sign of roof damage from in here, but I'll have my men give it a check anyway."

"I had the whole roof replaced about seven years ago," Mrs. Ravenhurst said, her expression severe. "I wouldn't like to have to speak to the owner of the company that installed it regarding the quality of their work."

"I don't think you need to worry about that," James said. "From everything I've seen, the roof is sound. But we will check it over just in case."

"That would be very good of you," Mrs. Ravenhurst said, once more serene. "Now come back downstairs, both of you. I'll have Doris make some coffee for us."

James gave Maggie a look, clearly impressed by the invitation.

"I hate to put you to any trouble," Maggie said. "I've already imposed on you more than I should have."

"Not at all. As you said, you needed to see the house so you'd know the type of things that would work in here. And it is nice to show it to someone who can appreciate what she's seeing."

They sat in the formal sitting room, enjoying coffee and petit fours and talking about the house. "It's all amazing," Maggie assured Mrs. Ravenhurst. "How much of it was passed down from the original Mr. Ravenhurst and his bride?"

"Quite a lot of it," Mrs. Ravenhurst told her. "Almost everything in my bedroom—the furniture, I mean—was theirs. And the formal dining table and chairs and sideboard."

Over coffee, she told them about the various pieces Ravenhurst had commissioned for the house and the more modern pieces she had gradually replaced with period ones that would blend in with the originals.

"You've done a fine job of it," Maggie said. "It's all gorgeous."

"Your Aunt Evelyn was a great help in that," Mrs. Ravenhurst said. "And June has been too. A few more pieces, and once we get the restoration done, I think it will be just right."

"I think the first Mrs. Ravenhurst would be very pleased with it all." Maggie hesitated for a second and then plunged in. "She must have led an interesting life."

Mrs. Ravenhurst nodded. "I believe she did. She was lauded as one of the loveliest and most accomplished ladies of her time. That's her portrait there. With her husband's."

Maggie looked where she had gestured and saw two oval-shaped portraits hanging one above the other in the narrow strip of wall between the two windows in the sitting room. She hadn't noticed them before, but they were quite striking.

Caroline Lacey Ravenhurst was fine-featured and delicate, her hair a soft gold, her skin rose-toned porcelain, her eyes vividly blue and of exceptional sweetness. Evander Ravenhurst was the ideal match for her. His handsome features were strong and lean, his hair a mass of tumbled dark curls pulled back into a queue. His eyes, dark and thickly lashed, were full of intelligence and humor.

"They're a handsome couple, though they look so much younger than I thought they'd be. I mean, I suppose I expected their portraits would have been done when they were middle-aged, when they'd established their family and all that."

"Her father commissioned the portraits for them as a wedding present," Mrs. Ravenhurst said. "They were done by an artist he'd brought all the way from London. They say he was especially pleased to have his daughter married so well."

"Especially after they had such a scare about her," Maggie said, as an open invitation for Mrs. Ravenhurst to tell her treasured story.

"Scare?" the older woman asked, one eyebrow arched.

"With the pirates and everything. I'd love to hear about it directly from you. I'm sure your family passed down some wonderful details about the incident."

Mrs. Ravenhurst stood, her expression abruptly cool. "I hope you will forgive me, but if you have both finished making whatever observations you need, I really have a number of things I must see to. Is there anything more about the renovations either of you need to ask me about?"

Dumbfounded, Maggie shook her head.

"I think I've seen what I need to," James told her, standing and pulling Maggie up next to him. "I'll get one of the men to inspect your roof right away."

"Thank you," Mrs. Ravenhurst said. "Do let me know if you find anything untoward."

"I will," James said. "Good afternoon."

He tugged Maggie's arm when she didn't immediately move.

Maggie gave Mrs. Ravenhurst a puzzled glance. "Uh, thank you for showing us the house. It really is lovely."

The older woman merely inclined her head slightly in response.

"Oh, I wanted to tell you we have a line on a pair of what look to be really nice armchairs. I can't say anything definite until I see them in person, but the pictures look very promising."

"And when do you think you'll be able to look them over?"

Maggie cringed inwardly, feeling as if she were standing before her first-grade teacher, expected to recite the alphabet without stumbling. "I have a call in to the estate agent that has them. I'm hoping I can go tomorrow."

"Very good," Mrs. Ravenhurst said. "Let me know what you think of them. Doris will show you out."

11

Maggie thought Mrs. Green must have been standing right outside the door of the sitting room because she appeared instantly.

"This way, please."

A moment later, Maggie found herself standing next to James on the front porch, Mrs. Ravenhurst's solid-oak front door firmly closed behind them.

"What was that about?" Maggie asked, stunned.

"Good question," he said as they walked down the steps toward his Mercedes.

"I thought she loved telling the story about how her ten-times-or-whatever great-grandfather saved his daughter from the notorious pirate and freed all of Somerset Harbor from his reign of terror."

"Her reaction was surprising. But we don't know for certain that's what set her off. It could have been something totally unrelated to the story. Did you slosh coffee in your saucer? Drop a crumb on your chair? Not cross your ankles while you were sitting?"

That teased a slight smile from her. "I was very careful to be on my best behavior."

"As you see, she can be a challenge. I'd suggest you not bring up the kidnapping or the pirate or the ring anytime soon. Not if you want her to keep patronizing your shop."

"I guess not. I don't understand what could have upset her about that old story. If I had asked her about her granddaughters, then I can see why she'd be upset. But this?"

"I don't understand it either. But you know, you were treading on thin ice when you asked about the kids' playroom up on the second floor. That used to be the girls' bedrooms and playroom before they left. She had my crew come in and redo everything in there about a week later. The *A*s and *R*s on those boxes on the third floor stand for their names—Amanda and Rachel. They're not Ravenhursts anymore, remember?"

Maggie glanced back at the house once they reached the car. "That's a pretty sad thing to cut family ties over, isn't it?"

"Probably just the last straw."

James reached to open the passenger-side door, but then he stopped.

"Excuse me a minute. I'd better get someone on that roof right away before I forget."

While he walked around the side of the house to talk to the foreman of his work crew, Maggie tried to think of another source of information about Solomon Zane and his ring. Even if she didn't get the original back, she at least wanted to know the story behind it and, if there was anything more to know, what happened to Zane himself.

"Hi there."

Startled, Maggie turned around to see a round-faced man in jeans and a denim jacket grinning at her from across the yard. He loped over to her, hedge clippers in one hand and the other outstretched.

"Did you come to see Mrs. Ravenhurst?" he asked, still grinning. "James is fixing the house for us, so that's why the work crew is here."

"He told me," Maggie said, returning the grin as she shook his hand. She had thought at first that he was very young, but now she saw he must be in his forties at least. "I'm Maggie. I'm helping with the furniture."

The man nodded, his face suddenly solemn. "We have to be careful with the good furniture. It breaks."

"Yes, some of it is very old."

Abruptly he grinned again. "I'm Hugh. I'm in charge of the yard work and some house stuff."

"Your mother is Mrs. Green, isn't she?"

He looked delighted. "Do you know her?"

"I met her a little while ago. I'm glad I got to meet you too. You keep the yard very nice."

He nodded. "Mrs. Ravenhurst trusts me to do it right. She has Jake check on it sometimes to be sure."

"Jake only helps you sometimes?" she asked. "It's a big yard."

"Yeah, but we do it right," he said. "Mostly me."

"Hey, numbskull!" someone called, and a tall, thin man strode around the corner of the house. "What'd you do with those—" He broke off, his pale eyes blinking, and then he ran his fingers through his wispy, straw-colored hair and put on a stiff smile. "You should have told me we had company, Hugh."

"Maggie's getting furniture for the house," Hugh said, beaming again. "She knows Mom and Mrs. Ravenhurst."

"I'm Jake Cobb, ma'am. I'm the groundskeeper and handyman around here."

"And me," Hugh insisted. "Mostly me."

"Mr. Cobb," Maggie said, glad the man didn't offer his hand. "Hugh tells me you help him with the yard here."

"I mostly do whatever Mrs. Ravenhurst wants. A nice lady like that needs looking out for, don't you think?"

"And we look out for her, don't we, Jake?" Hugh asked, looking at the younger man like an eager puppy.

"Yeah, sure, Hugh. Sure we do."

Two other men came around the house, rough-looking men covered with dirt. One of them was a lanky kid with sunburned cheeks and sun-bleached hair. The other one was older, dark, burly, and thick-necked. He briefly glanced at Maggie before turning to Cobb.

"Any luck?"

"Yeah," Cobb said, and he took the clippers from Hugh. "You and Tip see to the bushes along the east side of the garden and then get the roses done."

"Got it." The man tugged on the brim of his ball cap, the gesture somehow more disdainful than polite. "Ma'am."

"I was gonna do the roses," Hugh protested when the two men were gone. "You said I could this time."

"Better stick to mowing the grass for now," Cobb said, and then, with another glance toward Maggie, he gave Hugh a friendly swat on the shoulder. "I tell you what, when they get through looking at this part of the roof, you can clean out the gutters."

"Yeah." Hugh looked triumphant. "Yeah, I can do that." He took off and then stopped abruptly. "Bye, Maggie!"

Without waiting for her response, he tore off after the other men.

"I see you've met Hugh," James said, chuckling as he came up beside her, and then he sobered slightly. "And Jake."

"Mr. Bennett," Cobb said, briefly ducking his head. "I've been meaning to talk to you about those bushes around the foundation of the east wing. Mrs. Ravenhurst doesn't want to lose any of them, and we—"

"It's all right," James interrupted. "My men already know to be extra careful. If you'll keep your guys clear until we're done, that's the best help you could offer."

"I'll see to it." Cobb smiled his rigid smile. "Good to meet you, ma'am."

He strode off in the same direction Hugh had taken and disappeared.

James held the passenger-side door open for Maggie and then walked around and got behind the wheel.

"Now you're all up to date," he said with a grin. "What do you think?"

"I can't say I really liked anyone but Hugh."

"Hugh's a good man. He tries his best and has a great attitude. I'd like to see some others take their cues from him."

Maggie nodded. "I didn't like Jake Cobb at all. He's smarmy, like you said. Who was that other man, the burly one?"

"That was Cal Fisher. He and Dave Tippet do most of the heavy work around the place." James made a face. "I'm not sure I'd have Fisher or Cobb around if it were up to me, but it's not. And I guess they do all right. The grounds look like they're kept up, at any rate."

"Mrs. Ravenhurst must be satisfied with them, or I'm sure they wouldn't be here."

James chuckled. "You've got that right."

"I think," she announced as he buckled his seat belt and started the engine, "that I had better have a nice, long talk with Mr. Edmund Peters."

James looked unimpressed. "You don't really think that'll do you any good, do you?"

"I don't suppose I'll know till I talk to him."

"The man's a fraud. He doesn't do any actual research. Not with credible sources anyway. He finds a few names and dates and then makes up a wild story to go with them. He's as much a historian as I am a pastry chef."

"I don't know. He certainly acted like he knew something about that ring when he first came in to see it. Why would he bother if it didn't have some significance for him?"

"Who knows with that guy?" James pulled the car onto the road and turned toward the shop. "I think he's a little weasel."

Maggie chuckled. "Join the club. You don't believe he's actually dangerous or anything, do you?"

"Him? Nah. He's too much of a jellyfish to actually hurt anyone. I'd say he's more the type to sneak around, eavesdropping and stuff. I wouldn't put it past him to snatch something if he was sure he could get away with it. Besides, he's such a little worm, I think you could take him in a fistfight."

That made her laugh outright. "I'm so glad to know you have confidence in me."

"Anyway, my personal opinion is the less you have to do with him, the better off you'll be. But if you absolutely have to talk to him, I don't see any harm in it. Not that you have to listen to me in the first place."

She looked over at him. "I appreciate hearing your take on it. You've been around here a lot longer than I have, and you know the people a lot better than I do. But I think I'm going to call him."

. . . .

When Maggie got back to the shop, there was a message waiting for her from the estate agent. If she was willing to drive down to Stanhope around two in the afternoon the next day, she could inspect the pair of armchairs she was interested in. She called the number and made the appointment, glad at least something looked like it might pan out.

She spent the rest of the day helping June track down a Danish modern living room set and a rococo armoire. They finally found both in an auction house in Portland, but the house wouldn't sell anything except in person. Ah well, that would be another nice day trip. At least being in the antiques business didn't mean sitting behind the counter day after day.

She got home late that afternoon and was feeding Snickers when her phone rang.

"Hi, Mom!"

"Hey, Emily. How are you?"

"I'm good. I think I want to train to be an EMT."

Maggie blinked. "What?"

"You know, an Emergency Medical Technician."

Maggie shook her head, forgetting that Emily couldn't see her. "I know what it means. I didn't know you were interested in doing that, though. What brought this on?"

"My friend Tyler wiped out on his skateboard last night and had to have an ambulance and everything. I thought what the EMTs did was pretty cool. I'd like to do that."

"Is he okay?" Maggie asked.

"Oh, yeah. He broke two bones in his hand and has a lump on the back of his head, but he's all right. He didn't have to spend the night in the hospital or anything."

Maggie sat down on the couch, and Snickers immediately leapt onto her lap and started kneading. "That's good to hear. But are you sure about this EMT thing?"

"I think it would be great. I mean, I could be the difference between life and death for somebody. Right there on the front lines!"

Maggie cringed. She didn't want to dampen her daughter's enthusiasm, but there were practical considerations too.

"How are you going to have time for that?"

"I can take a night class. It won't be a big deal."

"I thought you were overwhelmed with the classes you already have. The last time I talked to you—"

Emily scoffed. "Mom, you worry too much. Last time we talked, I was stressed out. I had exams and stuff."

"What about your exams?" Maggie asked. "I thought you were going to let me know how you did."

"Oh yeah! Sorry, Mom. I did great on all of them. That one I had to take late, I still got an A on it, so it's all good."

Maggie exhaled. "Great. I knew you could do it."

"Yeah. It wasn't as bad as I thought."

Maggie grinned, glad to know Emily was in a better frame of mind than she had been, but still . . .

"So anyway, I think I'm going to sign up for the EMT training. I was thinking that since I'm already learning most of the stuff in my nursing classes, it won't be too hard. I'd like to get it all done at once."

"But honey—"

"Don't worry, Mom. I'm only going to check it out for right now. The class probably doesn't start till the summer session anyway."

"But what about the classes you have now?"

"Easy peasy."

Snickers had settled down and made one of his half-meow, half-purr sounds because Maggie had stopped petting him. She scratched behind his ears again. "As long as you don't fall behind in your regular studying."

"Nah, I won't. I just had to get through that first round of exams. I'm going to see that new zombie movie tonight."

"Oh, okay." Maggie turned her face away from the phone so her daughter wouldn't hear her nearly silent chuckle. Maybe she hadn't been too different at that age.

"How're you?" Emily asked. "Did you ever find out about that pirate ring? I'd love to see it. Jack Sparrow and all, you know?"

Maggie laughed. "That's what I've been saying."

Emily giggled.

"Anyway," Maggie said, "I haven't found out much more than I already knew. I got to go to Mrs. Ravenhurst's, and she was nice enough to show me all around the place. But she pretty much booted me and James out the door when I asked about the pirate kidnapping."

"Why?"

"That's the strange thing. Everybody I've talked to says she loves telling that story. I don't have a clue why she wouldn't this time."

"Does she know the real ring was stolen?" Emily asked. "Maybe she's mad she didn't get a chance to buy it from you or something."

"Hmmm, I doubt she knows about it. I guess she might be interested in it because of the family history. But I'm sure if she wanted it, she'd have made an offer and that would be that."

Emily considered for a minute. "What about that girl who sold it to you? Maybe Mrs. Ravenhurst knows who she is and doesn't want anyone else to find out."

"I guess that could be," Maggie admitted. "Seems a little far-fetched, but I suppose—"

"Ooooh, what if she's Mrs. Ravenhurst's secret daughter that nobody knows about?"

Maggie couldn't help laughing. "Honey, Mrs. Ravenhurst is probably eighty years old."

"Secret granddaughter then. Or great-granddaughter. You don't know."

"That's one thing I'm sure of," Maggie said. "I don't know much of anything."

"See?" Emily said, sounding suddenly sage. "But whatever it is, I bet it has to do with that girl. And I bet it's juicy."

"Don't you have some zombies to see?"

Emily took a startled breath. "Oh man, I'm gonna be late. Gotta go, Mom. Love you. Tell me when you find out something good."

Before Maggie could respond, the connection was ended. Shaking her head, she put down the phone.

"And that," she told Snickers, "is that."

Purring, he rolled over in her lap, displaying his round belly for her to scratch. She obliged him, thinking over what Emily had said about Mrs. Ravenhurst and Gail Lee. Secret granddaughter? Possible. Secret great-granddaughter? That was even more possible, and something Mrs. Ravenhurst would be much more likely to want kept quiet. Her granddaughters were in their thirties now according to James. They would have been quite young sixteen to eighteen years ago.

Maybe Emily was right and it was the girl and not the ring that was bothering Mrs. Ravenhurst. But where was Gail Lee? Or more importantly, *who* was Gail Lee?

And how am I going to find her?

12

As planned, Maggie made the drive down to Stanhope to look at the Queen Anne armchairs the following afternoon. As the agent had assured her, they were in excellent condition, and the price was surprisingly reasonable. Maggie bought them on the spot and arranged for them to be delivered to the shop. If for some reason Mrs. Ravenhurst rejected them, Maggie was certain another customer would be delighted to have them. There were several other items she decided to buy too, smaller ones that would easily fit in the backseat of her Jetta.

"Thank you," she told the agent once everything was packed up and securely stowed. "It's nice to find someone who has an eye for quality and isn't asking ridiculous prices."

The agent, a soft-spoken brunette still in her twenties, smiled shyly. "I'm trying to get established, and making customers happy is the best way, right?"

Maggie nodded, tucking the woman's card into her purse. "I'll certainly be calling you next time I'm looking for something specific. Thank you."

They shook hands and by four o'clock, Maggie was headed out of town. Stanhope was a small place, still with that mid-twentieth-century feel. She enjoyed the view as she sat at what appeared to be the town's lone traffic light, looking over the shops and restaurants around the main square. Maybe the next time Emily came home to visit, they could drive to the town, explore the shops, and have lunch at the little café on the corner.

The signal to cross the street started to flash, and Maggie got ready for the light to turn green. Suddenly a girl bolted out into the street in front of the Jetta. She was wearing a gray hoodie and had a backpack slung over one slender shoulder. Maggie blinked, not quite believing what she saw, and then she leaned her elbow in the frame of the driver's-side window so her hand would conceal her face as she watched the girl scurry to the opposite side of the street. An instant later, the SUV behind her honked, and Maggie was forced to move on.

I've found Gail Lee! Maggie turned around as soon as she was able and looked over the building the girl had gone into. The bus station. Was Stanhope the hometown she was leaving or a place she was heading back home from? Either way, if she got away this time, it seemed highly unlikely that Maggie would get another chance to talk to her.

She pulled into a little side street across from the bus station and parked. For a moment she sat scanning the sidewalks and the front of the station. Finally, she got out of the car and walked inside, trying to look as if she were there to catch the next bus to Portland. It took her only a minute to spot the girl sitting on a long bench in front of the windows. The people inside were too busy with welcomes and farewells, with baggage and tickets and snacks, to pay her or Maggie any attention.

Maggie stood for a few minutes, pretending she was looking at the monitors that showed the bus schedule but really watching Gail's reflection in the tall panes of glass. When she had come to the shop to sell the ring, she had looked nervous, even frightened. Now, more than anything else, she merely looked sad. She sat clutching that backpack in her arms, staring out the window, obviously seeing nothing. She didn't look at the passersby. She didn't seem to be waiting for anyone. She was alone.

Maggie watched for a moment more. Then, when a large, boisterous family came into the building, she seized her opportunity. There were at least a dozen of them, including several children giggling and jostling each other. One couple seemed to be the parents, but there were three or four other young adults and two elderly women. As they passed by, Maggie fell into step with them. When they swarmed past the girl's bench, Maggie abruptly sat next to her.

"Hello."

The girl turned, puzzled. Then her eyes widened and she tensed as if to bolt.

"Please don't run," Maggie said gently. "I don't want to have to call the police."

"P-police? I didn't do anything."

Maggie gave her a slightly dubious look, the same one she'd used on Emily over the past eighteen years when she knew her daughter hadn't been entirely forthcoming with the truth.

"You remember me, don't you?"

Gail nodded. "You work at the antiques shop in Somerset Harbor."

"I'm the owner," Maggie told her. "You sold me a very valuable ring for a lot less than it was worth."

The girl's mouth turned down. "That's not against the law."

"No. But replacing it with a fake later on certainly is."

The defiance in the girl's expression turned into bewilderment and then fright. "What? What do you mean?"

"That ring you sold me was definitely real gold and a real emerald. But a few days later I found out what I had was just a copy. A very nice one, I'll admit, but a copy all the same. I want to know what you know about it."

"That can't be right. I wasn't in your shop except that one time, I swear. I don't know anything about another ring. That's the only one I ever had."

"It seems a little odd that a few days after you sold me the real one, it was replaced with a perfect copy." Maggie made her expression stern. "Don't you think so?"

"I . . . I . . ." The girl glanced around the bus station, her eyes wide and bewildered. "Please, I didn't mean to do anything wrong, but I had to figure out some way to get out of here. I had to have some money." Finally she looked down at the backpack still clasped in her arms, and a tear slipped down her cheek. "Please don't get me in trouble."

"I think you're already in trouble, aren't you?" Maggie asked gently. "Why don't you tell me about it? Is it a boy?"

The girl's head jerked up, her face suddenly crimson. "No! No, it's nothing like that." Then she shrugged a little and looked away. "It seems so stupid now. I wanted to fit in with the cool girls, but there wasn't any way I could afford the kind of clothes and stuff they had. They said they couldn't either, and that's why they almost always stole stuff they liked. Shoplifted it."

It was the last thing Maggie had expected to hear, but she didn't interrupt.

"They said all the stores had insurance to pay for anything that got stolen, so it didn't actually hurt anybody."

"Except it does," Maggie told her. "Some places might not have that kind of insurance at all, and any losses come straight out of the owner's pocket. The ones with insurance wouldn't have to pay directly, but they would all have to pay in higher premiums over time. Either way, those costs get passed on to the customers in higher prices. So a lot of people who are struggling to make ends meet end up having an even harder time of it."

The girl looked stricken. "I . . . I didn't think of it like that. The girls said it was fun. A rush, you know?"

Maggie didn't know, but she nodded anyway.

The girl wiped her eyes on the back of her had. "Anyway, I did it a few times, but it wasn't fun at all. It was scary and I was afraid I'd get caught, so I told them I wouldn't do it anymore." She bit her lower lip and the tears welled into her eyes again.

"That's when they got really nasty. They said if I didn't steal stuff for them, they'd turn me in to the police."

Maggie frowned. "But if they did that, couldn't you turn them in too?"

"That's the thing, though. They didn't actually do any stealing. They got other girls to do it for them, and then they wouldn't let them out of it."

Maggie looked her over. Five hundred dollars and whatever she had crammed into that backpack was hardly enough to start a new life on. "So you're running away?"

"I have to. My mother would kill me if she found out what I've been doing or about the ring."

Now they were getting down to the real story.

Maggie laid her hand on the girl's arm. "Was the ring one of the things you stole?"

The girl nodded, again not meeting Maggie's eyes. "Sort of."

"Sort of?"

Shame colored the girl's face, and her eyes filled with unshed tears. "I took it from my mom's jewelry box. She doesn't have anything that's worth much, and that was the best thing in there."

"I see. Is that part of why you're running away?"

Again the girl nodded, her expression one of pure misery. "She's tried so hard to take care of everything since Dad died, and now I've made it all worse for her." She suddenly clutched Maggie's arm. "Please don't get me put in jail. Mom's having a hard time affording things as it is. She wouldn't be able to pay for a lawyer or to pay the stores back for what I stole. It'll be easier for her if I just leave."

Maggie looked at her and felt her heart breaking at the hopeless desperation in her young face. She clasped the hand on her arm.

"Do you really think making her sick with worry is going to make it easier for her?"

Bursting into tears, the girl tried to pull away from her, but Maggie put an arm around her instead.

"Why don't you let me take you home?"

"But my mother—"

"We'll get everything straightened out with your mother," Maggie soothed. "I'm pretty sure she'd rather you came back and told her what's happened so you can both figure out what to do about it."

"I'm so ashamed," the girl murmured. "Mom will never trust me again."

"Sure she will. If you tell her everything, if you tell her you want to make it right again, I bet she'll understand."

Again the girl wiped her eyes, this time on the sleeve of her hoodie. Then she looked warily at Maggie. "Why do you want to help me? You think I sold you a fake ring."

The corners of Maggie's mouth turned slightly upward. "Well, I would like to know what's going on with that ring, and I don't think I'm going to find out anything if you don't tell me about it."

A voice crackled over the loud speaker. "Now boarding No. 2534. The 2:20 bus to Los Angeles is now boarding."

The girl started, her eyes darting toward the door. "That's my bus."

"You don't really want to go, do you?"

A few minutes later, Maggie and the girl were driving down Stanhope's main street, away from the bus station.

"Your name isn't really Gail Lee, is it?" Maggie asked as they turned into a residential area.

"No. It's Abby Hawkins."

Maggie thought for a second. "The 'Gail' from 'Abigail'?"

Abby nodded. "And Leigh's my middle name, but it's L-E-I-G-H, not L-E-E."

"And your fake ID?"

The girl turned bright red. "My so-called friends told me how to get one. I guess I'd better get rid of it before it gets me into more trouble."

"Good idea," Maggie said. "By the way, I'm Maggie Watson. Now, why don't you tell me about the ring?"

Abby squirmed in her seat. "Mrs. Watson, I—"

"Call me Maggie."

"Maggie." Abby glanced at her out of the corner of her eye and then looked down at her lap. "I wish I could tell you about the ring, I really do, but I don't know anything about it. It's been in our family a long time. Mom had it in her jewelry box with my grandma's wedding ring, and I couldn't take *that*. I just couldn't." She swallowed hard. "I thought the gold ring would be the best thing to take. It would be worth enough to get me out to L.A. where I wouldn't be a burden to my mom anymore. The money I got for the ring would be a pretty good start out there."

Maggie cringed, imagining the girl all alone in Los Angeles with a mere $500. "Was I the first one you tried to sell the ring to?"

"Yeah. I thought Somerset Harbor was far away enough from here that nobody would recognize me. And I thought, in a small town, maybe people wouldn't ask too many questions."

"I should have asked more questions," Maggie said ruefully.

"I promise the ring I sold you was the only one I ever saw." The pleading in the girl's voice made her sound even younger than she was. "I don't know about any other ring, and I didn't take back the real one."

"I believe you," Maggie said, laying a calming hand on her arm. "But I don't know who switched out the rings or why." Recalling her conversation with Emily, she glanced over at Abby. "You don't happen to know anyone named Ravenhurst, do you?"

Abby looked puzzled. "Who?"

"Never mind. Tell me which way to turn when we get to the end of this street."

It wasn't an opulent neighborhood by any means, but being a widow herself, Maggie certainly understood about the financial hardships that often came with the grief of losing a husband. Abby's mother certainly didn't need to lose her daughter too. Maggie hoped there was some way she could help and that Abby's mother would welcome it.

13

A few minutes later, Maggie pulled into the driveway of a little single-story tract house with a patchy front yard and a struggling rosebush by the porch. Maggie followed Abby up to the door.

"It's going to be all right," Maggie told her when she hesitated. "I have a daughter not much older than you are. I might get mad at her sometimes, but that doesn't mean I don't love her. That doesn't mean I wouldn't do anything I could to help her. Your mother loves you, right?"

"Yeah. She does."

"All right then." Maggie gestured toward the house.

As if there were a firing squad awaiting her on the other side, Abby put her key in the lock and opened the door. "Mom?"

Maggie followed Abby into a small living room, neatly, if sparsely, furnished, with a little kitchen and dining area off of it. A door at the back of the kitchen evidently opened out to the backyard.

"Mom?" Abby called again. "Are you home?"

"In the office," a woman's voice replied from down the single hallway.

With a glance at Maggie, the girl disappeared and a moment later returned with her mother.

"Hello." The woman had the same petite build and dark eyes as her daughter and, though her hair was dark, there was a recognizable resemblance in her heart-shaped face. "Abby says you want to talk to me."

"Yes. My name is Maggie Watson. I own an antiques shop in Somerset Harbor, about twenty miles up the coast."

Abby's mother waited for her to go on, and her expression tightened. "Is something wrong?"

"Well, there's something you should know about." Maggie looked toward the floral-print sofa that had seen better days. "Maybe we could all sit down."

"All right."

"I think the best thing to do is just tell you straight out," Maggie said when they had settled on the sofa with Abby between them. "Recently, your daughter came into my shop to sell an antique ring, gold and emerald, with a sea serpent on it."

"Abby!" the woman gasped.

The girl ducked her head. "I'm really sorry, Mom. I know it was wrong. But I—"

Mrs. Hawkins laid a hand on Abby's arm to silence her. "I want to hear what Mrs. Watson has to say. Then we can talk about it."

Abby nodded.

"I could tell the ring was valuable, but I didn't want to buy it until I knew more about it," Maggie said. "So Abby and I agreed that I would give her $500 for it then, and later when I found out what it was worth, she could come back and either redeem the ring, or I'd pay her the rest of its value."

"I'm very sorry, Mrs. Watson," Abby's mother said, giving the girl a hard look. "But as you must be well aware, that ring is worth far more than $500. Abby will return the money to you, of course, but I'll have to have the ring back."

Abby squirmed in her seat, and her mother's look turned into a glare.

"You don't have the money anymore."

It wasn't a question.

"I didn't spend all of it," the girl said quickly. "Only about $200."

"Where in the world did you spend $200?" her mother demanded.

As simply as she could, Maggie relayed the story Abby had told her in the bus station.

"I know it was wrong," Abby added, sniffling. "But I didn't know how to get out of it. I thought . . ." Now the tears came in earnest. "I thought it would be better if I left so I wouldn't mess things up for you anymore. And then I even messed up that part of it."

"Oh, honey." Her mother wrapped her in her arms, pressing her cheek to the top of the girl's head. "You should have told me about it. We would have figured out what to do."

"I'm so sorry, Mom," Abby sobbed against her shoulder. "It was wrong to steal from the stores, but I feel worse about stealing from you."

"We'll get it all straightened out. Now the first thing to do is for you to give Mrs. Watson back whatever money you still have."

"I . . . I did that already. I gave her back the cash I had and the money for my bus ticket I didn't use."

Mrs. Hawkins turned to Maggie. "I'll make sure you have the rest of your money back as soon as I can. It might take me a little while to pay it off, but I will. You can keep the ring as security until I do."

Maggie winced slightly. "I'm afraid there's more, Mrs. Hawkins."

"Please, call me Kim. I think we're a little bit past being formal, aren't we?"

"I think so. Call me Maggie."

Kim nodded.

"Well, Kim . . . I don't have the ring anymore."

"What?"

"I can't give you a reasonable explanation for it. I tested the ring when Abby brought it into the shop. It was genuine gold and emerald. That's why I gave her the $500. I didn't expect to buy it for that, you understand. It was meant to be a down payment until I could find out more. But then I had an expert look at it, and he told me it was gold plate and green glass. Someone switched it out for a copy sometime after Abby left it with me."

Kim looked at her daughter with panic in her eyes, but the girl immediately shook her head.

"I swear, Mom, I don't know anything about that. I only took the ring out of your jewelry box. I never saw another one like it."

Kim patted her daughter's hand absently, looking as if she were scrambling to figure out what to do next. "I believe you, Abby. But . . . the ring is gone?"

She met Maggie's gaze, a sudden look of despair on her tired face.

"I'm sorry. I don't have an explanation for you. I can show you the replica. It's a very good one. My expert thinks it's from the mid-nineteenth century, so it wasn't made solely to switch out for the real one while it was at my shop."

Kim exhaled heavily. "I guess that's that."

"That ring is valuable," Maggie said. "Is it going to be hard for you? To lose it, I mean."

"Oh, I don't know." Kim looked bewildered. "It was my husband's. Passed down from some great-uncle or something. He loved that old thing. He liked to tell us it belonged to some bloodthirsty pirate back in the 1700s. I wouldn't have ever thought about selling it while he was alive because it meant so much to him, but now . . ." She lifted her chin. "He didn't have much insurance. Just a little from his job. He was only thirty-eight. We didn't think anything could possibly happen to him."

"I understand," Maggie murmured, knowing well how it felt to lose a husband without warning and far too early.

"I've been trying to make the insurance money last as long as I can. Sold the house and most of the furniture, moved here, sold the car and got a used one I could pay cash for, and got a second job doing accounting work at home nights and weekends." She patted her daughter's hand. "Abby's had to do without a lot of the things her friends have, but I thought we were doing all right. Now it turns out I have to put a new roof on the house and replace the timing belt on the car. Neither of those things can wait. I didn't have anything else to sell but the ring." She shrugged. "I guess I'll have to figure out something else."

"Maybe your family—"

"I'm afraid we're all we've got." Kim smiled tightly. "But that's not your problem. I shouldn't have told you all that anyway."

"I'm glad you did," Maggie assured her. "I feel terrible about losing the real ring, but I'm going to figure out what happened to it and get it back for you if I can."

"You haven't gone to the police?"

Maggie shook her head and glanced at Abby. "To be honest, I didn't want to get anybody into trouble over something that could be cleared up without involving the authorities. I have a daughter of my own, a little older than Abby, and I wouldn't want her to have to carry around a criminal record her whole life."

"I apologize that you got mixed up in all this," Kim said. "And thank you for being so understanding about Abby. Really, I'll make sure you get your money back, whether or not the ring is found. It's not your problem."

"I don't want you to worry about that right now," Maggie said. "It's not important."

"It *is* important," Kim insisted. "It's important to me."

Abby looked at her mother and then at Maggie. "Isn't there something I could do? I mean to earn the money I owe you? I could clean your house or run errands for you or something, couldn't I?"

Maggie thought for a moment. It would be good for Abby to take responsibility for her own missteps. "I think that would be an excellent solution if it's all right with your mom."

"I don't know," Kim said. "How would you get back and forth?"

"I could take the bus. It's about a five-minute walk from the stop to the antiques shop. That's how I got there before."

"I don't know," Kim said again, turning to Maggie. "Are you sure she could actually be of help?"

"It won't be a glamorous job," Maggie said with a grin. "But if you don't mind sweeping up and making coffee and unpacking boxes and that kind of thing, I wouldn't mind the help."

"I don't mind," Abby said, grinning back.

"Minimum wage," Maggie warned her. "And you'll have to work all day Saturdays."

"I can do that. Please, Mom. I'd feel so much better if you didn't have to worry about this too. And I ought to be the one to make it up." She clutched her mother's arm. "I feel so bad about everything. I thought you'd be better off if you didn't have me to worry about on top of everything else."

"Darling," Kim said, taking her daughter's face in both hands, "the only thing that's gotten me through these past two years is you. The worst thing you could do is take away the thing that keeps me going."

The two of them hugged tightly, and then Abby pulled away, a little self-conscious. "So, it's okay? If I work at the shop?"

Kim still looked rather reluctant.

"She can help me track down the real ring too," Maggie told

her. "I promise you I'm going to try my very best to find it and get it back for you."

"That would certainly be a relief," Kim admitted.

"It's the least I can do. It was in my custody when it was taken, after all."

Kim shook her head. "Please. I don't blame you at all. I actually wish I had time to help you. But if I don't keep up with my part-time work nights and weekends, I'll lose the little bit of extra money I get."

"Don't worry about it. Abby, when do you want to get started at the shop?"

Abby glanced at her mother. "Umm, now?"

Maggie and Kim both laughed.

"You're not behind on anything for school, are you?" Kim asked, looking as if she were trying to be stern.

"I have to read two chapters for my lit class, but I can do that tonight. Please, Mom."

"If it's all right with Maggie."

"I have a carload of antiques that are going to have to be unpacked when I get back to Somerset Harbor," Maggie said. "Of course it's all right with me."

Abby gave her mother a kiss on the cheek. "Thanks, Mom. I'll be home later."

Kim gave Maggie a half-bewildered, half-knowing look. "Are you sure you're up for this?"

"I told you I have a teenage daughter of my own. I've got this."

. . . .

After she and Kim had exchanged information—phone numbers, addresses, anything that might be needed in case of emergency—Maggie drove Abby back up to Somerset Harbor and pulled up in front of the shop.

"Okay, the first thing we need to do is unload everything. There's nothing really fragile, and everything's pretty well packed, but be careful anyway."

She and Abby both loaded their arms with bags and boxes and lugged them in through the back of the shop and into the storage room.

"Is that you, Maggie?" June called from the front.

"It's me."

June immediately popped her head into the doorway and gave the newcomer a surprised smile. "I see you brought back more than a few knickknacks."

"This is Abby. She's going to help us around the shop for a while."

June offered the girl her hand, her expression warm. "I'm June."

Abby looked a little uncertain, but she shook hands anyway. "Abby Hawkins."

"Good to have you with us, Abby. Now let me see what you two found."

"This isn't all," Maggie said, but before she could say anything more, Abby hurried to the back door.

"I'll get the rest. There's not much."

She disappeared, and June looked at Maggie, eyebrows lifted. "Where'd she come from?"

"It's the oddest thing. I was driving back from the estate agent's in Stanhope, and I saw her. She walked right in front of my car at a stoplight. She was on her way to the bus station, but I found her there and convinced her to go home instead."

June's forehead wrinkled. "So you hired her. You realize that makes absolutely no sense, right?"

"Oh. I forgot you didn't see her the first time she was here. That's Gail Lee."

June's eyes widened. "The girl who took your money, left

an expensive piece of jewelry that mysteriously disappeared, and then vanished?"

"One and the same. She'll be helping out until she can pay back the money I gave her. Shh, she's coming. I'll explain later."

Abby came in with her arms full, and Maggie and June helped her put everything down on the worktable. Before long, they had everything unpacked and listed for June to add to inventory.

"Now what do I do?" Abby asked, looking around. "I didn't really see much when I was in here before. You have some really cool things."

"We keep good track of them too," June said pointedly, holding up the list.

Abby nodded. "That's good."

Behind her back, Maggie scowled at June. Maybe Abby hadn't caught the subtle warning, but Maggie had.

"You don't need to worry about inventory," Maggie said cheerfully. "But the first thing I want you to learn is where we keep the coffee supplies and how the coffeemaker works."

Maggie took Abby to the coffee station by the sink in the corner of the room and showed her where everything was. But before she could give her instructions on how to make coffee, the girl had already begun the process.

"We have one exactly like this at home," Abby explained. "How do you like yours?"

Maggie gave June a smug little glance and then sat down, discussing the items she had brought back with her, where they could be displayed, and how they should be priced. It was nice when, a few minutes later, Abby brought them each a steaming cup of fresh coffee.

"I could get used to this," Maggie said, and then she sipped the coffee. "Ahh, that's great. Thank you, Abby."

Warily, June raised her mug to her lips. Then she looked a bit surprised. "Perfect. I'm impressed."

Abby shrugged, looking shyly pleased. "I'm glad you like it. Now what should I do?"

"You should make yourself a cup and come sit down," Maggie said. "Do you like coffee?"

"A little," Abby admitted. "I have some in the morning with my mom sometimes."

"Grab a cup if you want one, then come sit down. If we're going to get that ring back, we need to know everything we can about it and about anyone who might want it."

"But I told you," Abby said, a look of distress on her face as she sat too. "I don't know anything about it other than what my dad always said, but we always thought he was making it up. Or maybe his dad or granddad did."

"All your mother said was that he claimed it had once belonged to a pirate. Was there more to the story?"

Abby thought for a moment, a strand of blond hair twirled around one finger. "He always said somebody way back in our family had defeated the pirate in some kind of battle and took the ring from him and saved the town from being burned."

Maggie glanced over at June. The stories were similar enough. Could there be a connection?

"Do you know if the ring was passed down from his mother's side of the family or his father's?"

"I think he got it from his grandfather when he was in high school."

Maggie gave her an encouraging nod. "And was this his mother's father or his dad's?"

"His dad's."

"And do you know where *he* got the ring?"

Abby shrugged. "I guess from his dad or something. I don't know."

"So from the Hawkins line," Maggie said. "Right?"

"I'm sorry, but I don't know."

Maggie patted the girl's hand. "Don't worry about it. I'm wondering, though . . . are you sure there isn't anyone in your family named Ravenhurst?"

"Positive. At least not that I ever heard of," Abby said, her brows drawn together. "Do you want me to ask my mom about it?"

"Maybe, but not quite yet."

"Perhaps we could trace her family back on one of the ancestry sites," June suggested. "It might show a connection."

"Great idea." Maggie looked at Abby. "Would you mind if we did that?"

"I guess not. Is that going to help get the ring back?"

"I don't know." Maggie drank some more coffee, considering. "But if we know more about it, it might give us a clue about who might have taken it. There are things in the shop that are much more valuable than that ring. I don't think anyone would take it simply because it's made of gold and has a big emerald in it, not when there are so many other treasures here."

"But why else would anyone want it?" Abby asked, bewildered.

"That," Maggie said, "is what we're going to find out."

14

Before Maggie sent her new employee home for the day, she made sure to write down everything the girl could remember about the names of her grandparents and great-grandparents and where they were born.

"It's not much," Maggie told June when they were alone in the shop. "No Ravenhursts."

June glanced toward the door the girl had gone out, then rounded on Maggie. "Maggie, what in the world are you thinking?"

Maggie blinked at her. "That maybe we could find a connection between her family and Mrs. Ravenhurst's?"

June pursed her lips. "I mean what in the world are you thinking, bringing that girl to work here after she stole $500 from you?"

"But she didn't. She gave me a ring that was worth much more than I gave her."

"And then somehow switched it out for a fake one!"

"You don't know it was her," Maggie insisted. "You don't know that at all. Besides, she gave me back most of that money. She's going to work here until she can repay the rest."

"While robbing you blind."

Maggie shook her head. "I don't think she's the type."

"Are you telling me she didn't steal that ring in the first place?"

"Well, yes, she did. Sort of. She took it from her mother's jewelry box."

June put her hands on her hips. "And stealing from your own mother is better than stealing from a stranger?"

"I don't think either one is a good idea." Maggie sank into the straight-backed chair behind the cash register, exhaling heavily, and told June what had happened in Stanhope. "She's having a tough time right now. I can't help thinking that if Emily had been in a situation like this, I'd want someone to help her."

"She's not Emily," June said, her expression gentle and full of understanding now. "I know you miss having your daughter around, but you hardly know Abby."

"I'm not trying to replace Emily. I want to help Abby before she really gets herself into trouble. And I don't want you watching her every minute she's in the shop, like you're waiting to catch her doing something underhanded."

"But what if she is?" June asked. "What if all that in front of her mother, in front of you, was just for show? It got her out of trouble for what she did, and it got her another chance to take some things from the shop while she's working here."

"That's a long bus ride to take every day for someone who only wants to swipe some knickknacks, isn't it?" Maggie asked mildly.

"There have been more elaborate schemes than that for simple trinkets. Besides, some of those knickknacks are worth a good bit of money."

"I don't think Abby—"

"You don't *know*."

Maggie frowned. "You're right. I don't know. But until we know more, I hope we can make Abby feel as comfortable as possible. If she's telling the truth, she feels bad enough about what she did. We wouldn't want her to feel like nobody will ever trust her again or that she can't put this all behind her, would we?"

"I suppose you're right." June looked thoughtful for a moment. "But I still think somebody ought to keep an eye on her. Until we know her better."

"Fair enough. As long as she doesn't notice."

"Fine," June said. "But if you want her here, I think you'd better do the watching."

. . . .

"What happened to you?" Maggie gasped when Abby reported for work the next afternoon.

One corner of the girl's mouth was bruised and swollen, and there was a bandage wrapped around her right hand. Her eye was faintly blackened.

She shrugged, turning pink. "I feel so stupid. I got up in the middle of the night last night to get a drink from the kitchen and I didn't want to wake my mom. So I didn't turn on the lights. I thought I could feel my way, and I got all the way to the couch but forgot I had taken off my shoes when I was watching TV. I stepped on both of them and tripped." She held up her bandaged hand. "I hit the coffee table going down, and then Mom's paperweight fell off it and hit me in the face."

"Oh dear. You poor thing." Maggie shook her head. "Are you sure you're up to working today?"

"Of course. It doesn't hurt unless I smile." She tried it, winced, and then giggled.

Maggie chuckled too. "All right. I think June has something easy for you to do today anyway. June?"

June leaned her head out of the back room. "Hello, Abby. My goodness. I hope the other guy got it worse."

"There wasn't another guy, but I scared my mom half to death. She thought someone had broken in."

"Come on back here and have a seat. All you need to do is go through these packing slips and put them in chronological order, then file them. That doesn't sound too bad, does it?" June smiled sweetly at Maggie. "Didn't you say you would help with that? I mean, while I look after the front counter?"

Obviously, June didn't want Abby anywhere in the shop without supervision.

Maggie winced. "Actually, I thought I would go see Mr. Peters. He claimed to know something about that ring, but he wouldn't tell me. He said it would make me raise my price. Now that the ring's gone, there's no reason he couldn't tell me what he knows."

"Or what he's made up to tell you," June said.

"Either way, I'd like to hear it. Even made-up stories can have some truth in them. And since we know next to nothing anyway, I hate to throw away a chance to find out anything."

"I suppose that makes sense." June glanced at Abby and then looked pointedly at Maggie. "If you're going out, maybe you should go ahead and pick up those things we bought from Mrs. Benn's estate. It's a little farther down Shoreline from Peters's house. You can take Abby to help you pack everything up."

Subtle, June. Very subtle.

"That'll be perfect," Maggie said. "What do you think, Abby? Are you feeling up to it?"

"Oh, sure. I'm really fine. Do you think Mr. Peters knows where the ring is?"

"I don't know about that," Maggie said as they made their way out to the car. "But he was interested in it when it was at the shop. Maybe he'll tell us something that will help us figure out who took it."

They stopped at Mrs. Benn's house first. Her daughter, looking pale and tired, let them in and supervised as they packed up a very fine set of Spode china and some other small items. Then they headed over to Peters's house. He lived in a small stone house, more of a cottage really, that looked to have been built in the 1930s. The yard was rather overgrown and the house's wood trim was desperate for fresh paint, but otherwise it wasn't bad. Out front was a red Chevy Chevette, at least eight or ten years old, with a decal of a flag bearing the skull and crossbones. Peters's for sure.

Maggie picked up the package that had been left in front of the door and then rang the bell. After a moment, the lock clicked and the door swung open. Peters frowned at her. He had a cut over one eye, a bruise on his cheek, and a bandage across the bridge of his nose.

"What are you doing here?"

Maggie looked him up and down. "I'm sorry. Have I come at a bad time?"

"What do you want?" he asked, then glanced at Abby. "Who's that?"

"Abby's helping me at the shop. We really don't want to bother you, but you mentioned you knew something about that pirate's ring that was taken from the shop."

His eyes narrowed. "Come in."

He led them to a small living room sparsely furnished with midcentury pieces, but Maggie doubted most people would notice the furniture when the room held such an amazing array of old artifacts and curiosities.

"Wow," Maggie said, admiring a tiny cat, intricately carved out of jade. "I never saw so many beautiful things."

Peters's unshaven upper lip curled into a sneer. "I guess it was kind of hard to see it all in the dark like that."

Maggie frowned. "What?"

"You said you came to ask about that ring. I suppose you'd be surprised to know it was stolen last night."

"Stolen?"

Maggie glanced back at Abby, who merely looked bewildered.

"Oh, spare me the surprise. I was thinking you must have

had something to do with it, but I didn't think you and some *girl* would do the job yourselves."

"What in the world are you talking about?" Maggie demanded. "What happened to the ring? What happened to you?"

"I got a little bit bruised when you two locked me in my closet. It took a little while to work my way out. I ought to have called the police right then and there, but since there was just the one thing taken, I thought I'd see to it myself. I didn't know the two of you would come back."

"Come back? What do you mean? I've never been here before." Maggie turned to Abby. "Do you know Mr. Peters?"

"No," Abby said, eyes wide. "I've never been here before either. I've never seen him. I don't know what he's talking about."

Peters looked her up and down. "I thought I landed a couple of punches. I ought to have given you two black eyes instead of one, you little devil."

He lurched toward her, and Maggie stepped swiftly between them.

"Don't even think about it," she warned. "What exactly are you implying, Mr. Peters?"

"Look at her! Quite a coincidence that she's all bruised up today too, isn't it, Mrs. Watson?" Peters's wide mouth turned up in a sour sneer. "How do you explain that?"

"I fell." Abby held up her hands in a gesture of helplessness. "I tripped in the dark last night, that's all."

Maggie put both hands on her hips. "Don't be ridiculous, Mr. Peters. Look at her. She probably doesn't weigh a hundred pounds, and you're saying she overpowered a grown man and threw him into a closet?"

Peters stuck out his chin belligerently. "I was sound asleep and didn't know what was happening. I was disoriented."

Maggie looked at him dubiously, and he glared back at her.

"Besides, there were at least two of them. She wasn't alone." He lifted one thick eyebrow. "As you well know."

"So what are you saying, Mr. Peters? That Abby and I broke into your house, overpowered you, and stole the ring—that you apparently stole from me?"

"I'm saying exactly that. I ought to call the police and have them haul you both off. It's an outrage."

"Do you hear yourself? You've just admitted that you stole the ring in the first place! I'd say that was the outrage in this scenario, wouldn't you?"

His lower lip thrust out in a frustrated pout. "I tried to buy it. I made you a good offer, and you know it."

"You made me a pitiful offer. Fifteen hundred? Please. And no matter what you offered, that didn't give you the right to steal the ring when you knew I couldn't sell it. How'd you get it, anyway?"

He lifted his shoulders briefly. "Could have been switched out when the old Ravenhurst bat came in. That sort of thing would only take a second. If I did it, which I'm not saying I did."

"You just said that you did a moment ago."

"Try and prove it."

Maggie felt her exasperation with the man reaching new heights. "Okay. *Whoever* switched out the ring happened to have a perfect replica on hand to replace it with. I find that pretty interesting. Would you have any insight about that?"

"No." He bared his teeth slightly. "And I'm not saying it happened that way, and you can't prove anything anyway."

Maggie silently counted backward from five. She would not stoop to the man's level or let him push her to losing her temper. "I want to know what you know about that ring," she said firmly. "I want to know everything or, so help me, I'll call the police and let them see what they can prove."

He crossed his arms. "They might want to have a word with the both of you for breaking and entering. *And* for stealing my ring."

Maggie's mouth dropped open. "What?"

"*My* ring, Mrs. Watson. I bought it more than ten years ago from a dealer in Portland. I still have the receipt if the police need to see it. *One antique ring, gold plate, imitation emerald, sea serpent, crossed cutlasses, inscription on the inside.* It's all there. My ring. You've spread it all around town that you have it in your possession. I'm sure the police would like to know how it came to be there."

For a moment Maggie was speechless. He had clearly put the fake ring in place of the real one the last time he was in the shop, and now he was going to claim Maggie had stolen it from *him*? That she and dainty little Abby Hawkins had overpowered him to steal a ring that was green glass and gold plate?

Maggie pressed her lips into a hard line. "Edmund Peters, you are every bit the miserable little worm I was told you are. Do you really think the police are going to believe you?"

"There's her." He jerked his stubbled chin toward Abby. "What are they going to say about those bruises?"

The girl shrank back, and Maggie swallowed what she had been about to say. She couldn't let Abby get dragged into this. Not if the police were going to be involved. Then the story about Abby's shoplifting would come out. After that, who knew what consequences she might face? Then again . . .

Maggie looked at the girl out of the corner of her eye. It *was* quite a coincidence that Abby happened to trip and fall and get herself all bruised the very same night Peters's house had been broken into. It seemed ludicrous, but could he be right? She didn't know enough about any of this to risk telling the police. Not yet, anyway.

"You're right," she told Peters. "It is quite a coincidence that you'd both have a spill on the same night. Like it's quite a coincidence that the real pirate ring disappeared after you were in my shop the last time. Maybe the police would like to ask you about that."

For someone who had more or less coolly admitted to theft, Peters looked gravely offended that his integrity would be called into question. "I haven't been in your ratty little shop since that day Mrs. Ravenhurst was in. And you can't prove I took anything, then or after."

"And how do we know anyone ever broke in here?" Maggie asked. "Maybe you tripped over your coffee table too."

"Oh yeah?" He stalked over to the window at the back of the living room. "What do you think did this? Termites?"

She followed him across the room and looked where he was pointing. Someone had pried up the window frame enough to get to the latch and let him- or herself in. It could have been faked, she supposed, but it was pretty convincing. As were Peters's bruises.

"All right," she said tightly. "Let's be honest with each other. You came by the shop after June contacted you, asking about the ring, right?"

For a moment, he said nothing, his jaws clenched. Then he nodded. "I've been trying to find out about Solomon Zane for a long time now and got nowhere. The description sounded like a ring he was known to wear, and I wanted to see it."

"You wanted to steal it, you mean."

"I tried to buy it from you," he said, the picture of disdain.

"We won't go into that again. Now when I wouldn't sell, you decided you'd switch it for the fake ring, am I right?"

He looked down his nose at her. "I suppose it's a possibility."

"The ring you bought in Portland ten years ago."

"I told you I was interested in Zane, Mrs. Watson. If I could track down what actually happened to him, I could write a book about it. The replica was the first thing I'd ever come across that had anything to do with him, so I bought it. But then, when I thought I could have the real thing, I . . . well, if I were the type to bend the law a bit, you'd understand how I wouldn't have been able to help myself, right?"

"So you stole it."

Peters grinned faintly. "Your words, not mine."

"Hypothetically," Maggie said, frustration in her voice. "You came back with the replica and, when you got your chance, switched it for the real one. And then what happened?"

His heavy brows came together. "Nothing until last night. I was sound asleep, and then suddenly someone threw the bedspread over my head and hustled me over to the closet and locked me in." He glared at Abby.

"I swear it wasn't me!" She looked pleadingly at Maggie. "Honest. I didn't have anything to do with it. I just brought you the ring. The real one."

Maggie looked at her for a moment and then at Peters. It was crazy, but somehow she believed both of them.

"And you're telling me the truth, Mr. Peters, when you say you haven't been searching around my house or my shop?"

"Why would I? I already had what I wanted." Again he smirked. "Hypothetically."

"Well, I was nowhere near here last night," Maggie assured him. "I promise you, I have never been to your house before now, inside or outside."

He took another sidelong glance at Abby but didn't say anything.

"It seems to me," Maggie continued, "there's someone else interested in that ring. If it's not too much of an imposition, why don't we sit down, and you can tell us everything you know about the ring and about Solomon Zane. Then maybe we can get some idea about who else would be interested enough in the ring to track it down and steal it from you."

He took a deep breath, then nodded. "I'll tell you the absolute truth, Mrs. Watson. Believe it or not, I don't know any more about Solomon Zane than you do. I've been through all the records I can find. The replica of the ring was the only thing I ever found related to him, and the man I bought it from didn't know who had owned it before he did. He said it had been in his shop since his father's time and maybe before. The way Mrs. Ravenhurst tells it, back in the 1720s, Mr. Lacey and his boys dispatched the old pirate and that was that. Why don't you ask her about it? She's always happy to talk about how great her family is."

"I tried that already, and it was a disaster. She closed up like an angry clam and pretty much dismissed me."

"Did she now?" Peters asked, looking puzzled and intrigued all at once. "Did she really?"

"Yes. Why do you think she'd do that?"

"I really couldn't say." He took Maggie's arm and turned her toward the front door. "You might want to ask her."

"Wait a minute," she protested as he hustled her out with Abby scurrying after them. "Is that all you can tell me? When you were in the shop, you sounded like you had a lot of information you were keeping to yourself."

"I knew whose ring it was and you didn't. That's about all." They were on the front porch by then. "All I can tell you now is that somebody took the ring last night, and if it wasn't you two, I don't know who it was or why."

"That was my mom's ring," Abby said. "She needs the money from it really bad, and we need to get it back."

"Bad enough to break in?" he sniped.

Maggie laid a hand on the girl's shoulder. "Come on. We're not getting anywhere with this." She gave the man a hard look. "I'm not through with you, Mr. Peters. And I'll be keeping my eye on you. If I find out you know more than you're saying, I promise I'll go to the police."

"Look, lady, all I was interested in was finding out what happened to Zane and being the first to put out a book about him. People like pirate stories. They like mysteries. Throw in a little history, a little debauchery, and you've got a best seller. Now, I need a best seller, Mrs. Watson, and the sooner the better, so please don't get in my way."

"After that," Maggie said, "I thought it would be best if Abby and I left."

James reached across their table at The Lobster Quadrille and squeezed her arm. "I think it would be best if you stayed as far away from him as possible. Now don't you think you ought to at least talk to Robert Linton about this? If only to get his opinion."

Maggie winced slightly. Robert had helped her with sticky situations in the past, but she still needed to find out more before she involved him. "That's probably what I should do, but I can't bring myself to involve the police yet." She took another bite of lobster lasagna, savoring the tender chunks of lobster blended with spinach, at least three kinds of cheese, and an Alfredo sauce to die for.

"The man practically threatened you," James protested. "He's obviously a thief. What more do you need to know?"

"But it's not like he's habitually a thief. Well, not that I know of. He clearly wanted a keepsake in this case. I get the impression that he wants to be the go-to guy for all things Solomon Zane."

"Do you think he's really going to write a book?" James asked, raising an eyebrow as he cut a bite of fish.

"I don't know why not. He writes a blog. He must know something about writing."

James grinned. "Have you read some of the blogs out there?"

She wrinkled her nose at him. "He must do all right at least. He has companies who buy ad space from him. He gets a lot of hits and a lot of comments."

"Most of them telling him he's full of bull, I bet."

"I suppose any notice is good notice in that business."

They paused to thank the waiter who brought them a basket of fresh garlic bread and refilled their coffee.

"I did get the impression he was serious about the book," Maggie continued when they were alone again. "He seemed awfully determined that he was going to be the one to find out what happened to Zane and have exclusive access to the story." She pointed at his plate with her fork. "How's the haddock?"

"It's fine," he said, but he didn't look as if he was enjoying it at all. "I really wish you'd steer clear of him. He's got some kind of obsession with this pirate and having his exclusive best seller and all that. No telling what he would do if you interfered with his plans."

She was about to laugh it off, but then she heard Peters's words again as clearly as if he were at the table with them. *Don't get in my way.*

"It's ridiculous," she said. "No matter what he finds out or how much he doctors it up, he can't really expect to have a best seller, can he? Writers are like actors. Most of them have to have day jobs to keep food on the table. A few make a reasonable living. But the ones who actually hit the jackpot are few and far between."

James ate a few more bites of fish, alternating them with some of his seafood pasta salad.

"What about the girl? Abby. Do you believe her story?"

"I think so," Maggie admitted. "It does seem like a pretty big coincidence that she would hurt herself the same night Peters gets robbed, but good heavens, a strong wind would blow her away. How could she possibly overpower him?"

"And this other person Peters said was there? He or she could have been the burly one."

"True." Maggie speared a piece of steamed broccoli with her fork. "But then how would Abby have gotten bruised?"

"Right." James ate in silence for a moment, thinking. "If it was her—" He held up a hand to silence Maggie's protest. "*If* it was her, who do you think could have been in on it with her?"

Maggie rearranged the food on her plate distractedly. "I don't know. If she has been involved with a gang of shoplifters, I suppose she could have gotten one of them to help her."

"Another teenage girl? I guess it's possible, but it doesn't seem too likely either. Now, maybe if it were a grown woman . . ." He trailed off, looking at Maggie significantly.

She frowned. "I don't know what you're getting at."

"You told me how desperate Abby's mother was when you talked to her. If she's hurting for money that badly, who knows what she might do? That ring was hers. Peters stole it." James shrugged.

Maggie opened her mouth to argue and then shut it again. It was certainly possible. What did she know about Abby or her mother? What did she *really* know?

"I don't think so," she said at last. "She didn't seem the type to me. Besides, how would she know about Peters in the first place? It's not as if we put up wanted posters for him with directions to his house."

"I guess that's true." James took a bite of garlic bread. "And Peters couldn't tell you anything else about his burglars?"

"No. He's decided Abby was one of them, and evidently that settles it for him." Maggie hesitated, not wanting to remind him of her visit to the Ravenhurst mansion, but then she plunged ahead. "He seemed to think it was interesting that Mrs. Ravenhurst suddenly didn't want to talk about her family history. Do you have any idea why she would be that way?" Maggie let a little bit of a twinkle come into her eyes. "By the way, I didn't get you fired or anything, did I? I mean, later on?"

"Nearly." He pretended to scowl, and then his expression turned more thoughtful. "No, she didn't say anything else about it, but it's really hard to tell about her sometimes. You don't think she's after that ring, do you?"

Maggie immediately shook her head. "I considered that, but if she was, why wouldn't she simply buy it? She could afford to pay whatever Abby's mother wants for it, no questions asked. I can't see her breaking into someone's home to steal it."

"No, it wouldn't be much like her, you're right. I suppose she might be interested in it because it's connected to her family history, but if she stole it, she couldn't very well show it off later."

"Oh, speaking of family history," Maggie said, "I made a very interesting discovery when I was tracing Abby's ancestry. I was wondering how that ring might have been passed down to her mother, and what do you know? Abby's great-great-great-grandmother's name was Ruby. Ruby's maiden name was Ravenhurst."

James nearly choked on his coffee. "You're kidding."

"Not at all. Ruby and Mrs. Ravenhurst's great-grandfather, Philip, were brother and sister. If that ring was taken as some kind of trophy by the man who killed Solomon Zane, I guess it's perfectly possible that it made its way to Ruby Ravenhurst and then all the way to Abby. But that still doesn't tell us who would want to steal it or why. The one with a real motive so far is Peters, and he doesn't have it anymore."

"You *think* he doesn't have it anymore. What if the claim that it was stolen from him is a ruse so the rightful owner won't be able to ask for it back?"

"But wouldn't that spoil everything for him too?" Maggie asked. "He couldn't brag about it then. Or put it on his website. Or on the cover of his book or anything."

"And yet," James said, pointing a forkful of haddock at her, "he stole the ring in the first place. Those things must not have been all that important to him after all."

"That's true. Maybe he's like those people who buy stolen works of art and then keep them hidden. And maybe what Peters actually wanted was the knowledge that he had the ring that had once been Solomon Zane's, and bragging rights don't really matter. Then I guess we're back to him faking the theft so he wouldn't have to return the ring. How in the world do you prove something like that?"

James raised an eyebrow. "I think you tell the police about it, and let them handle it."

Maggie shrugged in response and toyed with what was left of her steamed vegetables. They had gone cold.

16

"Do you think I ought to go to the police?" Maggie asked June abruptly as they went through a box of embroidered linens and handmade lace the next morning. "About Peters and the ring, I mean."

"I don't know how it would hurt." June frowned at a stain on the corner of a cutwork piece with a basket of roses stitched on it and then put the item in the pile away from the ones in better condition. "Maybe James is right. You should at least talk to Robert Linton about it. That's not the same thing as filing an official complaint."

"I know. But Robert is probably going to tell me I ought to file an official complaint. And he'll want to know all the details, and then he'll want to talk to Abby about what happened with her so-called friends and the shoplifting, and that will be another mess on top of this one."

"You know best," June said dubiously. "So what are you going to do?"

"I still think Peters knows more than he's telling. He was vague about whether or not he took the genuine ring, but he more or less admitted it. *Hypothetically.*" Maggie wrinkled her nose. "But then I mentioned that Mrs. Ravenhurst hustled James and me out of her house when I asked about the pirate and the kidnapping. Peters gave me a look that made me think he knew something about that. Or maybe he thinks she knows more than she was ready to talk about."

June began unfolding a set of table napkins with a delicate border of embroidered leaves and flowers along the edges, inspecting them for damage. "That seems obvious from the way she reacted in the first place."

"True. But as weaselly as he is, Peters is the only one besides Mrs. Ravenhurst herself who might know why that was. And I suppose the best way to find out is to ask him about it."

June's eyes widened. "You're not going back out to his house, are you?"

"No. Not without James or a police escort or something. But I thought it wouldn't hurt to call him up and ask him about it."

June looked unconvinced. "And why would he tell you anything this time? Didn't you say he wants to break the big news about Zane?"

"He definitely wants to do that, and I don't care whether or not he does. But I want to know what happened too. And I want to get that ring back for Abby and her mother. Besides," Maggie said, "I also have to write that little article for the historical society's website about Zane and what happened to him."

"Peters won't like the idea of you stealing his thunder after he's been trying to find out about Zane for so long."

Maggie rummaged through the box as she thought for a moment. "Well, what about this? What if we agree that *he* can write the article for the historical society? That way he gets all the credit, the society gets its article, and everyone gets to know what happened to the notorious Solomon Zane. Everybody wins, right?"

"I guess there's no harm in trying."

Maggie chuckled. "You can stand right here when I call to make sure I'm safe."

June picked up a rolling pin that had to be close to two hundred years old and pretended to be fierce. "Just let him try something."

It took a moment for Maggie to find Peters's number, and with June standing guard, Maggie dialed his number.

He answered on the second ring. "What do you want?" he snapped when she identified herself.

She forced herself to remain pleasant. "I have what I think is a reasonable way to resolve the question of Solomon Zane's ring and, perhaps, keep everyone happy in the process."

There was a moment of silence. Finally, Peters said, "I'm listening."

"Look, I get that you want to break the story about Zane, whatever it is, and write your book and post on your blog and all that wonderful stuff. I'm fine with that. I'm interested in what happened to Zane, but just out of curiosity. I don't have any plans to commercialize the story. If you want to, go right ahead."

"And . . . ?" he asked when she paused for a moment.

"At this point, what I want to do is get that ring back for Abby's mother. She needs the money, and she's the rightful owner as far as I can tell. I couldn't sell it to you, because it wasn't mine, but she wants to sell. If you're willing to give her a reasonable price, I don't know why she wouldn't sell it to you. That's what you want, isn't it? And this way you wouldn't have to keep the ring hidden for the rest of your life."

"All right," he said, sounding a bit more interested. "What do you want from me? I don't know where the ring is. That's God's own truth."

"You know more about the ring, and about Solomon Zane, than anyone else. You've been trying to hunt him down for years."

There was a touch of bitterness in his faint laugh. "I told you, I don't know much more about him than you do. All right, I can tell you a bit about his life and about his infamous career all along the Maine coast and in other places. But I can't tell you what happened to him when he disappeared. I haven't found anything but a lot of conjecture, and I certainly don't know what happened to that ring. If you and that girl didn't take it, well, I'm sorry for suspecting you, but I don't know who else might have known I had it. I don't know where it is or who'd really want it that bad. It's a nice bit of jewelry, I'll grant you, but I'm not interested in it for that. And whoever took it must have wanted it because of whose it was, because there are things worth a lot more in my house that the burglar could have pocketed with it."

"Yes," Maggie said. "I saw them. You have quite a collection."

"Yes. I do." She could almost see the smug look on his face when he said it. Then he sighed. "I've spent a good part of my life looking for interesting historical objects and finding out the history behind them. I don't like it when I run into dead ends."

"I suppose that would be frustrating. But I'm hoping that we can get past this dead end and actually find out something. And I hope it's something that will give us an idea of who might have taken the ring."

"So what is this grand plan of yours? And why would you want me in on it?"

Maggie glanced at June, who was trying to follow the conversation from the half she could hear. June gave her an encouraging look, and Maggie drew a deep breath.

"When Abby and I were at your house, I mentioned that Mrs. Ravenhurst had turned very cool when I brought up the subject of the pirate and the kidnapping. I could tell that interested you, and I was hoping you'd tell me why."

"She's always liked telling that story," Peters said. "Makes her feel better than everyone else, right? I thought it was a bit strange that she would suddenly not want to tell it."

"Exactly. We all thought the same thing, but since you know more about it than we do, I was thinking maybe you had an idea why that was. Why would she be bothered by a story that's nearly three hundred years old, one that she's told at least a hundred times around Somerset Harbor?"

"I can't say for sure," he said, the words coming slowly.

"But I was trying to figure out what might have changed, you know? What is she doing now that she hasn't done before?"

Maggie thought for a moment, and then her eyes widened. "The restoration work! She's having things done all over her house. The east wing has practically been dismantled. There's no telling what she might have turned up during all that."

"That's what I was thinking. She must have found something—some old papers, a Bible, letters, anything with information about the family. There's no telling what she got ahold of or why she wouldn't want anyone knowing about it."

"Do you think she would really be that upset over some kind of scandal that long ago?" Maggie asked. "She's very proud of her family history, but—"

"'Very proud' is an understatement. Nobody had better even suggest there might be anything less than pristine in that bloodline." He snorted. "I made the mistake of asking her once if a second cousin of hers might have been a bootlegger, and she nearly tore my head off."

"Could it be as simple as she doesn't want anyone to know the girl's father and brothers disposed of Zane without a trial or anything like that? I suppose that would technically be murder."

"Nah," Peters said. "They'd have considered it justice back in the day, and to hear Mrs. Ravenhurst talk about it, she feels the same way. It's a point of pride for her."

Maggie exhaled heavily. "You don't have any brilliant theories about what she could have found, do you?"

"Not really."

"I guess it wouldn't do much good to come right out and ask her," Maggie said wistfully.

Peters barked out a laugh. "You can go ahead and try. Last time I asked her anything straight out, she threatened me with a lawsuit."

Maggie winced. "I guess that's that. It's only a theory anyway, and if she doesn't want to tell, I guess there's nothing that says she has to."

"I don't know," Peters said, his voice becoming even more smug than usual. "I didn't get ahead in my business without knowing how to get the information I need."

She knew he couldn't see her, but she glared anyway. "You're going to get yourself into trouble one day, Mr. Peters. Mrs. Ravenhurst is very rich and very well-connected. Are you sure you want to get on her bad side?"

"I've never been that concerned about whether people like me, Mrs. Watson."

Obviously. "You'd better be careful all the same," she said aloud. "And you'd better hope we track down that ring. Otherwise, I really am going to have to tell the police you stole it from my shop."

"Good luck proving that," he said, his tone almost jaunty. "But I do like the idea of buying it from the lady when it turns up. I'd like to have a picture of it on the cover of my book."

Maggie looked at June and rolled her eyes. June lifted her eyebrows and shook her head, since she couldn't hear what Maggie was hearing.

"As long as you give her a fair price," Maggie said into the phone, "that's fine with me. Speaking of writing though, I was asked to write a piece for the historical society website about whatever I found out about Zane. I know you want to be the one to write about him," she talked over him as he began to sputter, "so if you want to write the article for the site, that would be fine with me. You can be our guest expert."

"What? And spoil the big revelation in my book?"

"You don't have a book yet."

"*When* I have a book."

"I'm sure the society doesn't want a pseudo-advertisement for your book on their site. Though if we did post the article, it would probably generate interest in Zane and maybe in your book."

"Not if you tell everybody what happened to Zane right up front," Peters protested. "So I guess it's a race to see who finds out first. I plan for that to be me."

"Mr. Peters, don't—"

Silence. He had ended the call.

"—get yourself into trouble," Maggie finished, looking uncertainly at June. "Oh boy."

17

"What did he say?" June asked when Maggie put down her phone. "I got most of it from your side of the conversation. Sounds like he doesn't really have a clue either."

"No," Maggie admitted. "Not much of one. All he said that was useful was that maybe Mrs. Ravenhurst has discovered new information about her family from something she found while the house is being renovated, and she wants it hushed up."

"Why does he think that?"

"Something must have changed to make her not want to tell her pirate story anymore."

June thought for a moment. "What if it wasn't anything to do with the house? What if it was the ring itself?"

"What do you mean?"

"The ring has been more or less lost all these years," June said. "At least as far as Mrs. Ravenhurst is concerned. She probably never even knew there was a ring in the first place. And now, out of the blue, this one shows up. You start asking questions about her family. Peters gets interested in Solomon Zane again. Couldn't that be all there is to it and nothing to do with the renovations?"

"I suppose that's possible. But what does the ring mean to her? How could people asking about Zane reflect badly on her or her family? It's well known that he existed. That ring doesn't prove anything about what happened to him or whether or not Mrs. Ravenhurst's ancestor was responsible for his death. It has to be something more than that. Something to do with her family and not Zane himself."

June frowned. "Like what? And what would the ring have to do with it?"

"I don't know. It has to be something Mrs. Ravenhurst wouldn't want anyone to find out about." Maggie lifted one eyebrow. "Maybe some scandal that's bad enough to make her take matters into her own hands."

June's mouth dropped open. "Did he say he thinks *she* stole the ring from him?"

"No," Maggie said, thinking. "Not really. Not outright. But seriously, who else would care about the ring? He said whoever stole it must have wanted it because of its history, and I think he must be right. He had several more-valuable things out on display at his house. A thief who was interested in money would have taken them too."

"I truly can't imagine her overpowering Peters and shoving him into his closet," June said, clearly trying not to giggle.

"She wouldn't have done it herself, silly. However, she could certainly afford to pay to have it done. But why?"

"I think your theory is right. It has to be something that affects her family," June said thoughtfully. "She's always been very prideful about being in a direct line to the first Ravenhurst and how the Laceys could be traced back to the *Mayflower*. Could she have found out something shocking about that?"

"I can't help wondering if it might have something to do with Abby being around Somerset Harbor now."

June looked puzzled. "Abby?"

"Oh, I don't think I told you this part. Back in the Ravenhurst family tree, about 150 years ago, there were a brother and sister. Mrs. Ravenhurst is descended from the brother. And Abby—"

"Is descended from the sister!" June crowed. "Well, that's a juicy little connection. But what would that have to do with Solomon Zane? He wasn't in her family line. He wasn't—"

Maggie's breath caught. "Oh."

"What?"

"Oh my."

"Maggie, what?"

"I just had an awful thought about the girl who was kidnapped by Zane. Suppose she didn't escape as unharmed as her family claimed."

"What do you mean? Oh." June's eyes widened. "You don't think there was a baby, do you?"

"There could have been. If even half of what they say about pirates and captive maidens is true, there very well could have been."

"But she would have been ruined. No matter that it wasn't the least bit her fault, she would have been absolutely ruined. No respectable man would have married her. The child . . . the child wouldn't have been received in polite society, though it would have been the most innocent of all."

"I know. It wouldn't be at all surprising if the whole thing was hushed up. Then Ravenhurst comes into town, a perfect stranger, and meets her father in the course of business while the pregnancy isn't very far along. Her father sees he's a good catch and hustles them into marriage. And of course, captivated by her beautiful face and gentle demeanor, Ravenhurst doesn't object to his sudden good fortune. He's simply thankful that his premature child is so strong and healthy."

June shook her head. "That's a horrible story. And you don't have any more proof that that was the way it happened than you do of anything else."

"No, but it makes sense, doesn't it? Isn't that the kind of thing that Mrs. Ravenhurst would think would contaminate her pristine family history? If she was upset with Peters simply implying that a second cousin of hers was a bootlegger during

Prohibition, how do you think she'd react to finding out that she didn't have any of the vaunted Ravenhurst blood at all?"

"She'd still be descended from the girl's family," June offered.

"The Laceys were the ones with the *Mayflower* connection Mrs. Ravenhurst is so proud of, but that wouldn't make up for being descended from a depraved, murderous pirate. Not to Mrs.—"

"Mrs. Ravenhurst!" June jumped out of her chair and scurried to the door, opening it before Mrs. Ravenhurst could touch the doorknob. "Good afternoon. How are you?"

Mrs. Ravenhurst inclined her head slightly. "I am well, thank you, June. You seem flustered. Is everything all right?"

June smiled cheerily. "We've been rearranging the shop."

"I see." Mrs. Ravenhurst glanced around the shop and gave an approving little nod. "I must say you do an excellent job of it."

"Thank you, Mrs. Ravenhurst," June said, looking a little surprised at the praise.

"Otherwise I wouldn't bring my business here."

Maggie coughed to cover her grin, and Mrs. Ravenhurst turned a cool gaze on her.

"Good afternoon, Maggie. Are you all right? You look rather flushed."

"Like June said, we were working hard. Oftentimes we have to move things around quite a bit before we get all the pieces to fit together the way they should. Sometimes we're not sure we even have the right pieces. Speaking of the right pieces, I'm sorry to say we haven't found that sideboard you want for your dining room. Not yet, anyway."

"That's not a problem," the older woman said. "The Ravenhurst home has been there for nearly three hundred years. It will still be there when the right furnishings turn up. But that's not why I came to see you."

"Anything else we can find for you?" June asked, her notepad in hand.

"Actually, there's something you already have in the shop that I would like to buy."

"Excellent. Which piece are you interested in?"

Maggie's heart began to race when Mrs. Ravenhurst walked over to the display case that held the antique jewelry. There was only one thing she could be looking for there.

"You had . . ." Mrs. Ravenhurst squinted into the case and then she turned to Maggie. "You had a gold ring in here when I stopped by the other day. A rather large one with an emerald and with sea serpent on it. Probably from the early eighteenth century. Peters was looking at it. Is that still available?"

The woman's expression was perfectly calm and innocent. If she knew about the theft, especially if she had commissioned it, she was certainly not giving herself away.

"We *had* a ring like that, Mrs. Ravenhurst," Maggie said. "Unfortunately, it was stolen a few days ago, and I don't know where it is."

Mrs. Ravenhurst inclined her head. "Yes, I heard about that. I also heard that the genuine ring was replaced by an eighteenth-century copy. That copy is the ring I'd like to buy from you."

Maggie glanced at June and then looked at Mrs. Ravenhurst. "It's an interesting piece, but really, it's actually gold plate and green glass. I'm not sure why anyone . . ."

Mrs. Ravenhurst looked mildly amused. "You asked me the other day about the story of the pirate and Caroline Lacey. That ring, or at least the one it's modeled after, belonged to the pirate. It's part of my family history, and I would very much like to own it. I'll give you a good price for the piece—you needn't worry about that."

"To tell you the truth, Mrs. Ravenhurst, that ring belongs to Mr. Peters." Maggie tried to keep from wincing at the distasteful expression that name brought to the other woman's face. "He's letting me have it on . . . on loan for a while. I'm a member of the historical society, and they're interested in putting some information about Zane on their website, because he was part of our local history. We're both trying to find out what we can about the pirate and what might have happened to him when he disappeared. If there's anything you have to contribute to the article, we'd all be very grateful." Maggie managed a hopeful little smile despite June's warning expression behind Mrs. Ravenhurst's back.

Mrs. Ravenhurst's expression was as cold and stiff as marble. "If you're interested in anything remotely resembling historical fact and reliable research, I suggest you stay as far as possible from Mr. Peters. He's a troublemaker and a thief and a liar. He's not interested in history. He's interested in making a dollar, no matter how he does it, no matter what unfounded conclusions he leaps to."

Maggie tried her most appealing look. "I don't really know Mr. Peters, but I know he has that reputation around Somerset Harbor. That's why I thought you would want to tell us what you know about Zane and—" June was glaring at her now from behind Mrs. Ravenhurst's back. "—and everything that happened until he disappeared. That way we'll make sure to get it all right."

"No doubt you've already looked into the matter. There's nothing else to tell. Caroline Lacey was abducted from her bed by Zane and his cutthroats and held for ransom. Not long after, still with the ransom unpaid, she returned home unharmed and Zane was never heard from again. If her father and brothers brought him to a rough justice, I am certain it was richly deserved."

"I don't doubt it was," Maggie said. "But since he was a historical figure, it seems only right to tell his story."

"To me, since he was a pirate and a murderer and a cruel and evil man, it seems only right if, instead of glamorizing him, we leave him to be forgotten as quickly as possible."

Before Maggie could respond to that, the bell on the front door jingled and Abby came into the shop.

"Hi!" she called, shrugging out of her backpack. "Sorry I'm a little late, but the bus didn't come on time. Anyway, Mom wanted to know if you found out anything about—"

"Abby!" June said, hurrying to her. "We were starting to worry about you. Now that you're here, I have some things for you to do in the back. Remember that set of books we were expecting? They've come in and—"

"Who's this?" Mrs. Ravenhurst asked, looking at the girl over the frame of her glasses. "I didn't know you'd taken on extra help."

"It's a temporary arrangement," Maggie said. "This is Abby Hawkins. Abby, this is Mrs. Ravenhurst. She's—"

"She's one of our very best clients," June said. "She's the one who's purchasing those chairs we recently got in."

"I like your new chairs, Mrs. Ravenhurst," Abby said. "They're really nice."

There was something sweet and genuine in the girl's shy smile, and for a moment Mrs. Ravenhurst's stony expression softened.

"They are lovely, aren't they?" There was a sudden touch of humor in her eyes. "I'm glad you approve."

Abby ducked her head, but she looked up again when she saw the warmth in the older woman's expression. "I don't know anything about antiques, but I think your house is going to look really pretty when it's done. I got to unpack some of the stuff you ordered, and it's all so interesting. Not like new things that don't have any history."

"Perhaps next time Maggie or June comes out to my house, you could come along and see some of my other pieces. Some of them have been in the house for almost three hundred years."

"Yes ma'am, I'd like that very much."

Mrs. Ravenhurst nodded indulgently. "All right then. You run along and see if there are more of my things for you to unpack. I'll see you later on."

"Come on now," June said, and she and the girl disappeared into the back room.

Maggie hardly knew what to say. Who knew prickly Mrs. Ravenhurst had a softer side?

"As I was saying, Maggie, it would be best if Solomon Zane and his depravity were forgotten rather than celebrated."

The softer side was definitely gone now.

"I agree. We certainly wouldn't celebrate him," Maggie said. "But preserving the history of Somerset Harbor is important."

There wasn't a trace of agitation on Mrs. Ravenhurst's impassive face. "You may do as you please, as I am sure you will. But remember what they say about birds of a feather. If you insist on associating with people like Edmund Peters, I will have to wonder if this is the sort of business one should patronize."

Maggie's thoughts immediately turned to June. She certainly didn't want to be responsible for losing Mrs. Ravenhurst's business. "I understand how you must feel about your family history, Mrs. Ravenhurst. I didn't mean to upset you with all this."

The other woman looked faintly annoyed. "Don't be ridiculous. It was purely a word of caution you may either take or leave. Now, about the replica ring . . ."

"I'm sorry, but as I told you, it's not mine to sell."

Mrs. Ravenhurst's lips tightened into a hard line. "Mr. Peters. Yes, I understand. I would consider it a very great favor then if you would approach him on my behalf and ask if he would be willing to sell the ring and at what price."

"I will do that," Maggie said. It seemed little enough to appease the woman and, she hoped, keep her lucrative business. "But I should tell you that I don't think he wants to sell. He's been trying to find out what happened to Zane for over a decade now, and that replica is the one artifact he's found that's even remotely connected to him."

"Yes, I know about his second-rate little blog. Surely there are other things he could feature on it."

"I think he wants to do more than write about all this on his blog," Maggie told her. "He thinks that, if he can find out what really happened to Zane, he can write a book about the pirate's life and be the first to break the story about why he disappeared. Peters is sure he'll have a best seller."

Mrs. Ravenhurst's eyes were glittering and hard. "Oh, I'm certain he would. No doubt he'd add all kinds of scandalous details, whether they were true or not, that the public would eat up, and one cannot sue for defamation of the dead. Well, I won't—"

Abruptly, she snapped her mouth closed, but there were twin red spots on her pale cheeks, and her breath came in little puffs through her nose.

Won't what? Won't allow it? Maggie watched her, waiting for her to continue.

"I won't waste any more of your time, Maggie," she said finally. "If it's not too much of an imposition, I would still like you to ask Peters about selling me that ring."

"I'd be happy to do it for you, of course."

"Thank you." Mrs. Ravenhurst tucked her clutch purse under her arm. "Good afternoon."

With no more than the jingle of the bell over the door, she left the shop.

June immediately peeped out of the back room. "Did you make it out alive?"

"Barely." Maggie sank down into one of the chairs behind the counter. "I hope I haven't lost her business."

"It's hard to say," June admitted with a glance toward the door. "But it looked to me like she was going to deal with Peters herself if she needs to."

"She wasn't at all pleased. I can tell you that for sure."

"She seemed to like Abby," June said, taking the chair next to Maggie's.

"That was a bit of a surprise." Maggie glanced toward the back room.

June asked, "Do you think she might be thinking about an unacknowledged great-granddaughter?"

"Stranger things have happened, you know. But that doesn't explain why she wants to hush up everything about Zane. That wouldn't have the least bit to do with Abby, whether or not she's more closely related to the Ravenhursts than we know. Why didn't you let me tell her Abby has some Ravenhurst ancestors?"

"If you're right about what happened to Caroline Lacey, Mrs. Ravenhurst probably isn't in the mood to talk about family history. Besides, you haven't even told Abby about that yet, have you?"

"I hadn't thought of that. Maybe I should tell her now." Maggie considered for a minute. "Or maybe we'd better find out a little more about the family line first."

18

"All I looked at before," Maggie said as she pulled up the information she had found on the Ravenhurst family, "was the first Mr. Ravenhurst's line down to the current Mrs. Ravenhurst. She's as direct a descendant as you can get, father to son and so on until it got to her."

June squinted at the screen. "That is, if the first Mr. Ravenhurst was actually the father of the second."

"According to this, Evander Ravenhurst and Caroline Lacey were married in May of 1722. That was when the house was finished. Their first child, John, was born in October of 1723."

"And when was the kidnapping?" June asked.

"The summer of 1720. August, I think. Let me look." Maggie flipped open the little notebook she kept by the computer and nodded. "Yeah, August fifth was when she disappeared. She came back home on the twenty-first. So if there was a child involved, it would have most likely been born sometime around May of 1721, not October of 1723."

June frowned. "I suppose there could have been a child that wasn't included in the genealogy. Maybe her family made her give it up so there wouldn't be a scandal."

"Perfectly possible," Maggie said. "But it wouldn't be this child who was born in 1723, and who was the ancestor of our Mrs. Ravenhurst."

"They could have lied about the date that child was born."

"Not by nearly two and a half years." Maggie pulled up a photograph of the record showing the child's baptism. "And it would have been hard to sneak it into the list of the other baptisms on and around that date. It's not like typing it into a computer and making the other lines move down one to accommodate it."

"I suppose you're right. Drat. That would have explained things so nicely."

"Well, as awful as it would have been for the girl, there's no reason for Mrs. Ravenhurst to particularly want a secret child kept quiet, if that had been the case in the first place. She would still be descended from the very respectable Mr. Ravenhurst and the very from-the-*Mayflower* Miss Lacey." Maggie clicked on the photo of the couple's gravestones. "*Forever mourned.* That doesn't sound like something a man tricked into marriage would put on his wife's headstone. He loved her, and I would be very surprised if she didn't love him every bit as much."

"Could be," June said. "It would have been great if she had remembered what happened to her while she was on that ship, though. If she escaped somehow, especially if she was as unharmed as all the accounts say, it would be very interesting to know how she managed it."

"It would."

Maggie thought back to the portrait of the girl hanging in Mrs. Ravenhurst's sitting room. It was idealized, no doubt, but it was the undeniable sweetness in the eyes that gave her beauty far more than the dainty features depicted there. Was that how the girl had truly looked in life or something added by the artist's skilled hand? How could she have gone through such a harrowing ordeal and come out unharmed emotionally and physically?

"Whatever has upset Mrs. Ravenhurst, I don't think it's the idea that she is descended from a pirate's secret baby."

June giggled. "Wasn't that in one of the soaps a few years ago? Or maybe it was just a bad romance novel. *I Was a Pirate's Secret Baby.*"

"Stop it," Maggie said, giggling herself. "This is supposed

to be serious. What in the world could she have found out about Solomon Zane that she doesn't want to get out?"

"Wait a minute. What if Caroline was actually the pirate's secret baby?"

Maggie rolled her eyes. "Don't be silly."

"No, really. What if Zane kidnapped her for the ransom and then realized she was the spitting image of the woman he had left behind in the South Seas twenty years before?"

"That's really stretching, isn't it?"

"It would explain why he would let her go unharmed and without paying any ransom," June said. "Think about it."

"And how would this secret baby have ended up with the Laceys in Maine?" Maggie demanded, hands on hips.

"How would I know? Maybe this woman Zane left behind was Mrs. Lacey's sister who had fallen out with their father and broken their mother's heart. And then, when she was dying, abandoned and alone, she entrusted her loving sister with her newborn baby, begging her to raise the child as her own and never tell her of her shameful past."

Maggie pursed her lips. "That sounds like something straight out of a dime novel."

June grinned. "It's possible. If Caroline didn't have a secret baby, how else do you explain Mrs. Ravenhurst being so upset about this whole pirate thing? It almost has to be something about her ancestry. What else would matter to her at this point?"

"I guess it's possible," Maggie admitted. "But that still doesn't tell us what happened to the ring or the pirate."

"I don't know who's more likely to have the ring now than Mrs. Ravenhurst herself. If she wants Solomon Zane and every memory of him to disappear, she can afford to have someone see to it for her."

"But why wouldn't she just buy the thing?" Maggie leaned

her chin on her hand, thinking. "Unless she already tried to buy it from Peters and he wouldn't sell."

"Why in the world not? He could name his own price."

"Don't forget that best seller he's going to write."

"How could I?" June rolled her eyes. "So he'll be rich. Why not sell it and not bother with writing the book?"

"Except it's not just the money for him. He wants to be the great historian, the expert on something, even if it is simply a minor pirate and his mysterious disappearance."

June's expression turned grave. "You realize that if it really is Mrs. Ravenhurst who has the ring now, she didn't go over to Peters's house herself to steal it. She had to have somebody do it for her."

"Of course."

"The kind of men who do that sort of thing by request aren't people you want to mess with, Maggie. Maybe it's time you dropped this whole pirate thing and got back to business."

"But what about Abby's mother?" Maggie said. "She needs to get the ring back. She needs the money."

"Then she should go to the police about it and let them sort everything out."

Maggie shook her head. "She's not going to do that. She'd risk getting Abby into trouble for stealing it in the first place."

"Her mother wouldn't press charges for that!"

"No, but the police might find out why Abby was so desperate to leave home, and then there might be problems because of her shoplifting." Maggie frowned. "Besides, if Mrs. Ravenhurst denies knowing anything about the ring at all, she's more likely to be believed than anyone else in Somerset Harbor, isn't she? And we don't actually have proof that anybody did anything at this point."

"You know Peters stole the ring from you."

"I can't prove it, and he doesn't have it anymore. It would be his word against mine, and he doesn't seem the type to mind lying if it suits him." Maggie stood up and patted June's shoulder. "Don't worry. I'll be careful. But I really want to track down that ring and get it back to Abby's mom."

"I don't like it," June muttered, standing as well.

"If it makes you feel better, I'll have to put my sleuthing aside for a while anyway. Tomorrow's the auction in Stonebrook."

"I hate that you have to drive all that way by yourself," June said. "Why don't you take your protégé along?"

"Abby? Are you tired of watching her all the time?"

"I haven't been watching her," June insisted. "At least not after the second or third day she came to work here."

Maggie chuckled. "See? I told you she was a good kid."

"I guess so. At least so far."

"I think I will ask her to go with me, if it's all right with her mother that she's out late. It's not a school day, and Abby would probably like doing something out of the ordinary." Maggie thought for a minute. "I can't get over how much Mrs. Ravenhurst seemed to like her. I mean, at least as much as she likes anyone."

"It was surprising, that's for sure. Maybe after all these years she's missing those granddaughters of hers."

"Could be." Maggie thought again about the loveless mansion on a hill. "Maybe when all this is settled, she'd be happy to know she still has family in the area."

"Even if it is a fifth cousin."

"Third cousin," Maggie corrected. "Twice removed."

. . . .

The next morning, Maggie put a little extra food in Snickers's bowl and made sure he had plenty of water.

"I'll probably be late," she told him. "No wild parties while I'm gone."

He was too busy wolfing down his savory chicken-and-beef blend to make her any promises, and with a farewell pat, she hurried out to her car.

"Maggie!"

She turned and was delighted to see James jogging down Shoreline Drive toward her. "Hello, James. What are you doing here?"

"Finishing my run. How about some coffee over at The Busy Bean after I shower and change? My treat."

"I'd love to, but I'm headed to Stonebrook for an auction. There are several pieces listed that might be perfect for the Ravenhurst home."

He blotted his face with his sleeve. "That's a long drive. Are you spending the night there?"

"No, I'm coming right back. It probably won't be later than ten or eleven when I get home."

"I don't like you going all that way alone. Couldn't June go with you?"

"Somebody's got to run the shop," she reminded him. "But I'm not going alone. I'm taking Abby."

He cocked his head. "Abby? Who's Abby?"

Maggie realized she hadn't told him about the girl yet. "She's the girl who sold me the ring. I'm rescuing her from a life of crime by having her work at the shop for a while."

"That's good to know. I'd like to know the full story sometime."

"How are the renovations coming over at Mrs. Ravenhurst's, by the way? It looked like you had things pretty much torn up in the east wing when I was there. Your men didn't happen to make any interesting finds when they were taking down walls or anything, did they?"

James wiped his brow again. "Oh, didn't I tell you? They found the bones of Solomon Zane bricked up behind a fireplace. A dagger with the Lacey family crest on it was lodged in his spine."

Maggie tried to look stern. "It was not."

"It was," he insisted, a twinkle in his blue eyes. "And he had a piece of paper clutched in his bony fingers where he had written down all the details about how he died."

She snickered. "I take it that means no one has actually found anything."

"Sorry. The most interesting thing we've found in the walls so far was an old hammer and what's left of a carpenter's apron. Nothing about pirates or ransoms or anything." His expression turned serious. "Funny thing is that your Mr. Peters asked me very nearly the same thing yesterday."

"Did he?"

"I'm afraid I couldn't tell him any more than I told you. What's he after?"

"I wish I knew." Maggie glanced at her watch. "I have to go pick up Abby, so I can't really go into everything right now, but basically he thinks Mrs. Ravenhurst found something during the renovations that she doesn't want anyone else to find out. He's determined to find out what it is, of course. I hope he doesn't go too far."

James frowned. "I think Robert Linton ought to know about this."

"But Peters hasn't done anything."

"Yet."

She bit her lip. "You don't think Mrs. Ravenhurst could actually be in danger, do you?"

He shrugged, his grim expression softening. "I don't know. And if there was trouble, she has Jake Cobb and some of the other sturdy boys she has working around the place. They'd be there all the time, plus the work crew during the day. She'll be all right. And you'd better get going."

She checked the time again. "Oops. I'm running late. I'll talk to you later."

"Have fun, Maggie, and please be safe."

· · · · · · · · · · · · · · · · ·

Maggie and Abby had a pleasant-enough drive to Stonebrook, though Abby was more intent on playing games on her phone than making conversation. She took the news of her connection to the Ravenhurst family with no more than a placid "Oh. That's cool," but for several minutes afterward she sat in contemplative silence, her game abandoned, at least for the moment.

They got to Stonebrook after the auction had already started. The gavel was going down on the first item on her list, a Queen Anne chest of drawers. This one was in perfect condition, tall, beautifully made with carved-and-gilded shells and inlaid stars, and she winced when she heard the final price. It had gone for far less than Mrs. Ravenhurst had authorized. Things got even worse from there.

Maggie found that the gorgeous mahogany desk she coveted for the refurbished office was a replica. She was outbid on a pristine set of blue-and-white Staffordshire dishes that would have been perfect for the plate rail in the dining room, and she found that the gloriously carved French wedding wardrobe that was meant to be the centerpiece of the main bedroom in the east wing had been withdrawn from the auction at the last minute. All in all, the whole day was a colossal failure. At least she and Abby enjoyed a delicious dinner at a little Chinese buffet on the way back and even spent a few minutes feeding the koi.

Maggie wasn't in the best of moods as she drove through Somerset Harbor on her way to take Abby back home. The girl said she'd been up late the night before helping her mother around the house, so she was curled up in the passenger seat, asleep. Maggie couldn't help smiling wistfully at how young she looked. Like Emily when she was younger. Tears sprang to Maggie's eyes and she dashed them away, laughing softly at herself. She was pretty tired herself. It hadn't been much of a day, and she was ready to go home and get into a hot bath.

It was nearly eleven, and there wasn't much traffic on the road as she took the curve that brought the Ravenhurst home into view. It loomed black at the top of the hill, with a few security lights outside the place. Mrs. Ravenhurst would be disappointed that Maggie hadn't come back from the auction with any of the items they had discussed. Had she really arranged to have that ring stolen? It seemed incredible, but who else would want it besides Peters?

She passed the house and started down the hill. *Wait. Peters drives a red Chevy Chevette, doesn't he?*

Maggie swerved over to the side of the road and stopped. With a little gasp, Abby pushed herself up straight and blinked at Maggie.

"What happened? Are we home?"

"Not yet," Maggie said, turning out the headlights. "I want to know what's going on here."

The girl gaped at her and then looked around. "Where are we?"

"That's Mrs. Ravenhurst's house." Maggie pointed up the hill behind them. "And that is almost definitely Mr. Peters's car."

Blinking again, Abby looked at the car parked a few feet ahead of them. It was well off the road, almost in the trees. "I remember that pirate flag sticker from when we were at his house."

"I thought that was his. I wonder what he's doing here."

Abby yawned and rubbed both eyes. "Maybe he came to talk to Mrs. Ravenhurst about that pirate."

"Then why would he park out here on the highway away from the house?"

Abby shrugged.

Maggie looked around. There was a house across the street and about a hundred yards down with the porch light on. She pulled up into the driveway.

"I want you to stay here. I'm going to go up to Mrs. Ravenhurst's house and make sure there's nothing strange going on. If you see anything, or if Mr. Peters comes back to his car before I get back, you call 911, okay? If you need to, lean on the horn. That'll get somebody's attention."

Abby nodded. "Are you sure you should do that? Go up there, I mean."

"I'm only going to take a look. You stay here, all right? And keep the doors locked."

"But Maggie—"

"And keep your phone handy." Maggie rummaged in her purse for her own phone and then got out of the car. "Lock the doors," she told Abby again. And once she heard the locks click, she headed up to the house.

The moon shone barely enough to keep her from stumbling as she made her way through the trees on the back side of the hill. There was a little bit of a wind, so the branches and leaves swayed and rustled, covering, she hoped, the sound of her steps in the grass. She didn't think her breathing was usually uncommonly loud, but somehow it seemed so now. Surely someone would hear her. And if Peters was up to no good—

She stopped, partly concealed by a tree. There was a light on the first floor in the east wing. There hadn't been anything a moment ago. It was just a pinpoint, perhaps a flashlight, but it was definitely there. If that was Peters, what was he doing? If Mrs. Ravenhurst had found something, perhaps it had been found in the east wing. It was the most torn up at present. Most of the rest of the house had only superficial renovations being done.

The light moved, now a mere glow inside the empty room. She thought Peters must be standing between the light source and her. She took the opportunity to move closer, all the way up to one of the glassless windows. Even in the dimness, she recognized the hunched shoulders and stocky build, the lank dark hair and the furtive way of moving. It was Peters all right.

She froze when another light flashed on. Then she heard an angry male voice.

"What are you doing here?"

"What are you doing here?" the man demanded again. "What do you want?"

Peters swallowed hard, his face pale even in the dim light, but Maggie couldn't tell much about the other man. The other *men*, she realized as she inched closer. There were two of them she saw now, Jake Cobb and the other man she'd seen when she came with James to see the house. Fisher. They might not be the most savory characters, but they were certainly capable of protecting Mrs. Ravenhurst's home. *Good,* Maggie thought. They'd see Peters off without much argument.

"It's that Peters, Jake," Fisher said. "The one who's been upsetting Mrs. Ravenhurst."

"Oh," Jake said, and his slash of a mouth twisted up. "It's you, is it? I'd have thought you'd know better than to be putting your nose in where it doesn't belong."

Peters took a step back from them. "You . . . you're the ones who broke into my house."

The two men looked at each other.

"We heard you ran into some trouble the other night, Mr. Peters," Fisher said. "Heard you got a little roughed up. That's a pity."

"But we'd never do anything of the kind," Jake said. "Would we, Fisher? Mrs. Ravenhurst wouldn't like it."

Peters shrank back a little, saying nothing. Maggie felt her heart racing against her rib cage. She didn't know whether she ought to creep away from the house and drive off or call the police. After a moment's indecision, she took out her phone and started recording.

"Of course not. But if somebody was to break into this house . . ." Fisher shook his head regretfully. "Having your nice home broken into and things taken from it? It's unsettling. You wouldn't want a nice lady like Mrs. Ravenhurst to go through that, would you?"

"That old bat," Peters muttered.

Fisher lurched at him and grabbed him by the front of his shirt. Maggie flinched. She had to do something before this got really ugly.

"I'll have the police on you," Peters whimpered. "I swear I will."

Jake rubbed his heavy fist contemplatively. "I don't know that the police would blame us if we were to have to protect Mrs. Ravenhurst from someone breaking into her house in the middle of the night. What do you say, Fisher? They'd thank us, wouldn't they?"

"Give us a medal, I'd say," Fisher replied.

"I'll tell them," Peters said, his voice a high squeak now. "I'll tell them what you did. I'll tell them you broke into my house, stole my property, and assaulted my person."

"That'll be a little hard for you to do, Mr. Peters," Jake said solicitously. "Your teeth being smashed in and all."

"You wouldn't dare," Peters squeaked. "You wouldn't—"

"You wouldn't want to be arrested for assault," Maggie said, projecting a coolness she did not feel. She held up her phone as she stepped through the low window and into the dim circle of light cast by Peters's flashlight. "I've been recording everything you've said and done. If anything happens to me or to Mr. Peters, the police will know exactly who to blame."

Fisher and Jake looked at each other, and then a wicked grin turned up the corners of Jake's mouth.

"Looks to me like you're trespassing too, lady. Maybe you'd better give that phone to me, and then we'll see what ought to happen to you both."

Heart pounding, she took a step backward and stumbled over a two-by-four. Jake caught her by the upper arm, snatching her phone from her as he did.

"You give me that!"

To her own ears, her voice sounded high and thin, as terrified as Peters's had been. Surely they wouldn't actually hurt her. Jake held the phone well out of her reach, chuckling as she struggled to get it back.

"Give it back!"

"First we have to talk about this little recording you made."

He looked around the torn-up room and spied a hammer that one of James's workmen had left behind on a sawhorse. Still holding her by the arm and grinning, he set her phone on the sawhorse and picked up the hammer.

Maggie's eyes widened. "Don't you dare."

Jake glanced at Fisher who stood smirking back at him and raised the hammer.

"No, Jake! Don't!" Maggie turned to see Hugh Green hurry through the door, a plastic baseball bat clutched in both hands. "Don't hurt Maggie. You can't hurt her."

"What are you doing up?" Jake growled. "I thought your mother told you to stay out of this wing while it's being worked on."

"I know." Hugh ducked his head a little. "But I had to get a drink and I heard you over here. You gotta let Maggie go. A gentleman never raises his hand to a lady."

If she hadn't been so scared, Maggie's heart would have warmed at that. It was something her father and grandfather had always said. Something too rarely seen these days, it seemed.

Jake sneered. "You get out of here, Hugh. I think your mother wants you."

Hugh put back his shoulders and stuck out his chin. "She

does not. She's asleep. You let Maggie go. And Mr. Peters too." He shook one thick finger at Peters. "You shouldn't be here. You don't belong here. Not unless Mrs. Ravenhurst invites you."

Peters scowled. "Those two broke into my house and stole something from me, not to mention assaulted me. I ought to go to the police."

Jake released his hold on Maggie and lurched toward Peters. "Why you little—"

"No!" Hugh stepped between them, pulling Peters out of Jake's reach. "No, stop. It wasn't them, Mr. Peters. Honest. It was me."

Maggie gasped. The other men gaped at Hugh.

"You did?" Maggie whispered.

Hugh nodded, his eyes on the bare floor. "I just wanted to help. Mrs. Ravenhurst was so upset about that ring thing and—"

"What is going on here?" Finding her way with a flashlight of her own, Mrs. Ravenhurst stepped into the disheveled room, wrapped in a green velvet dressing gown, her white hair loose and flowing to her waist. Her bare feet were covered by little silver bedroom slippers. "What are you doing?"

Hugh gaped at her. "I, uh, we—"

"I'll tell you what's going on, Mrs. Ravenhurst." Maggie snatched up her phone and shoved it into her pocket. "Though I suppose you already know."

"What do you mean?" the older woman demanded. "What is all this?"

"You had Hugh break into Mr. Peters's house and steal that ring," Maggie said, anger now taking the place of fear. "Now Peters has come here to find out what you're trying to cover up, and you sent your men out to scare him off, rough him up if need be."

Mrs. Ravenhurst's eyes were blazing. "How dare you make such a ridiculous accusation? Hugh, release that man at once. What are you doing?"

Hugh let go so quickly that Peters nearly fell on his face.

"Hugh assaulted me, Mrs. Ravenhurst." Peters drew himself up with as much dignity as he could muster. "I don't like to be blunt, but there it is. He and one of your other men broke into my home and took my property, all on your orders. Don't think you can cover it up." He glared at his now-tame assailants. "Don't think I don't know who runs the show here."

Mrs. Ravenhurst looked from him to Maggie and then at Hugh. "Hugh, I want to know what you have been up to. No, don't tell me it was nothing. I want to know what you've done. Right this minute."

Hugh glanced at Peters and then looked at the floor, his hands clasped in front of him. "We—Tip and I—we did what we thought you wanted. Mom said you were worried about that ring and didn't want anyone else to have it, so we thought we'd get it back for you."

"I see. And where is the ring now?"

"We—we put it up so it didn't bother you anymore." Hugh gulped. "We didn't hurt him, not really, and we didn't take anything else. We were trying to help. And then I heard noises out here and came to see what it was and Jake was, um, talking to Mr. Peters and Maggie, and I thought they should go home."

Jake merely stood glowering and said nothing.

Mrs. Ravenhurst fixed him with a baleful eye and then turned again to Hugh, her expression softening, if only infinitesimally. "You go back into the other part of the house and tell your mother what you've done. I'll come and talk to both of you later."

"Aww," he muttered, his lower lip wobbling, but then he shuffled away.

When he was gone, Mrs. Ravenhurst's expression turned steely once more. "As for you, Jake, I want to know exactly what you and Fisher are up to."

"We heard somebody rustling around in here and thought we ought to see who it was. We found Peters rummaging through things and then this lady showed up threatening us with the police and I don't know what all. That's as much as I know about it."

"And you know nothing about Hugh breaking into Mr. Peters's home?" Mrs. Ravenhurst asked. "You weren't part of that? Fisher?"

"No ma'am," Fisher said. "Nothing like that."

"Not us, Mrs. Ravenhurst," Jake assured her, "and that's the plain truth. Just now's the first we heard of it. We were only trying to do our jobs and deal with intruders."

"Very well then. You two go on back to bed. I'll see to this."

Jake glanced at Maggie, and she stared coldly back. Peters looked smug. Defeated, Jake clenched his jaw and stalked off with Fisher in his wake.

"I'm rather surprised to see you here at this hour, Maggie. Surely it cannot be about the sideboard you were trying to find for me."

Maggie's face turned hot. "No. I happened to be passing by and saw Mr. Peters's car out behind your house. I wanted to make sure he wasn't causing you any problems."

"You could have as easily rung the doorbell." Mrs. Ravenhurst turned to Peters, her arms crossed as she looked down on him with an icy expression. "Precisely why are you in my home, Mr. Peters? I can hardly imagine Jake and Fisher dragged you here for some nefarious reason."

His catfish mouth turned down. "All right, I was trying to figure out what you found. I know there's something, so there's no use denying it. You found something in all this rubbish, and I think it has to do with Solomon Zane and that girl he kidnapped. She was your ancestor, right? You wouldn't want anyone to find out something, oh, I don't know, *unsavory* about the sainted Ravenhursts?" He raised one heavy black brow. "What was it? Did you find out she wasn't kidnapped? That she ran away with him, so her father hunted them down, murdered him, and dragged her back?"

Maggie's eyes widened. She hadn't thought of that. A beautiful young girl like that, enamored of a crusty old pirate? Stranger things had happened, of course, but what an idea. The secret-baby theory suddenly seemed more plausible.

Surprisingly, Mrs. Ravenhurst laughed. "That is quite possibly the most ludicrous thing I have heard in all my considerable years. No, Mr. Peters, I have not the slightest bit of evidence that that was ever the case. I can tell you without a doubt that Caroline Lacey loved her husband from the time she met him until the time of her death. Solomon Zane? Good gracious, never in a million years."

"Then what was it?" Peters demanded. "I have a right to know. Somerset Harbor has a right to know!"

"Somerset Harbor has a right?" Mrs. Ravenhurst's gray eyes blazed. "*You* have a right? All anyone has a right to know is their own business. Nothing about my family is anyone's business but my own."

Peters glared at her defiantly. "That half-wit, Hugh Green, helped rob my house. From what he said, it's obvious he still has the ring. Unless you tell me what you know about Solomon Zane, I might have a few charges to press myself."

"You stole that ring in the first place," Maggie snapped at him. "Haven't we had this conversation already?"

Peters shrugged. "It might be that when I was comparing

my copy with the original at your shop, the two got mixed up. It's an easy enough thing to do, wouldn't you say? If you had come and asked me about it when it first happened, we might have gotten the problem sorted out right away. But then Mrs. Ravenhurst had to have her thugs ransack my home and, well, what am I to do?"

The little weasel. He changes his story as often as it suits him.

"And your reason for breaking into Mrs. Ravenhurst's home?" Maggie asked, her mouth tight.

"To get my replica back, of course. Hugh stole it and brought it here. I want it back." Peters was the picture of innocence. "I had no way of knowing it was the genuine ring and not mine, now did I?"

"And how did you know it was Hugh? You certainly didn't know or even suspect he was involved when I talked to you last."

Maggie could see him scrambling for an answer.

"Well—well, who else could it be but somebody who worked for Mrs. Ravenhurst?" he blustered.

"Am I correct that you have possession of the replica, Maggie?" Mrs. Ravenhurst asked.

"Yes. It's at my shop."

"If that was returned to Mr. Peters, he would have no more legal interest in the matter, would he?"

"I don't think he would," Maggie replied in mock thoughtfulness. "Unless he was thinking about pressing charges against Hugh and your other man, Tippet, and that would open a can of worms he would have a difficult time closing."

"Very difficult." Mrs. Ravenhurst looked pointedly at Peters. "Can you really afford to be tied up in court for the foreseeable future?"

He gulped.

"Lawyers are notoriously expensive, and then there's

the matter of your reputation in general versus my own." Mrs. Ravenhurst lowered her voice conspiratorially. "I know a lot of people, Mr. Peters. Many of them in positions of influence. Do you think it's worth it? Whatever you think you might profit from any story you think I might be able to tell you, do you think it's worth it?"

"Solomon Zane might be of interest here in Somerset Harbor," Maggie added. "Maybe even in Maine in general. But it takes a lot more than Maine to make a best seller. There are a lot of writers in the world, and very few actually make a living off their craft. Do you really want to challenge Mrs. Ravenhurst and her very expensive attorneys in court for the minuscule chance that your book about a local pirate will be a national success?"

He pressed his lips into a hard line, saying nothing. "Then I want to write that article for the historical society with the information I already have, with links back to my website and all that. At least I could get a little publicity from it."

"The historical society site doesn't sell ad space," Maggie told him sharply.

He considered for a moment longer, and then he huffed. "Then I want the real ring. That's fair, considering the gold mine I'm giving up. I'll keep my mouth shut about all this for Solomon Zane's genuine ring."

Maggie chuckled sardonically. "Yet again, Mr. Peters, that ring doesn't belong to me. Or to Mrs. Ravenhurst. If you have the money, I know the owner wants to sell. Can you afford it?"

His shoulders drooped. "All right. I'm done. I can't fight you and your money, Mrs. Ravenhurst. You keep your secrets. I won't bother you anymore."

Mrs. Ravenhurst inclined her head. "You're a wiser man

than I thought you were. And perhaps, if I see you're behaving yourself, I will tell you some of the stories of some of my antiques and you can use them on your blog. I assure you there are some very interesting ones."

He looked at her suspiciously. "Really?"

"*If* we have an understanding."

"All right," he said with a grudging nod. "Fair's fair. You know how to reach me when you're ready."

She gave him another of her cool smiles. "Good night, Mr. Peters. I trust you know your way out."

He recognized the dismissal and, with a curt nod, stepped over the low windowsill and disappeared into the darkness.

The moment he was gone, Mrs. Ravenhurst put one hand to her mouth and her eyes filled with tears. She was no longer a queen of ice and steel, but a woman, frail and old. Maggie went to her and took her arm, certain she would be rebuffed. Instead, Mrs. Ravenhurst clung to her, trembling.

"Poor Hugh. I never told him to do such a thing. You must believe me, Maggie. I've been so upset by all of this, and I know he realizes it, poor boy, but I never told him to go steal that ring. It's monstrous. To think I might have had to appear in court over such a charge—it's unthinkable."

"I believe you," Maggie said softly. "Whatever's bothering you, will it help to talk about it?"

"Mrs. Ravenhurst?" Doris Green hurried into the torn-up room also in her robe and slippers, though her yellow chenille and fuzzy pink house shoes were much more plebeian than her mistress's. "Oh ma'am, Hugh told me what he did. It's my fault, I'm afraid. I'm so very sorry."

Mrs. Ravenhurst shook her head. "No, I can blame no one but myself. For all of this." She fumbled in the pocket of her robe and brought out an embroidered handkerchief, which she used to blot her tears. Then she patted Maggie's hand, releasing herself. "I think I can trust you."

Maggie nodded. "You have my word. Whatever it is, I won't tell anyone. Ever."

Mrs. Ravenhurst led Maggie over to the fireplace. Several of the stones had been removed.

"They're going to take all of this down, clean up the stones, and then replace them with new mortar. They were about to fall in, and the fireplace wasn't safe to use. They took down the mantel too." She shone her flashlight on the long piece of beautifully carved wood, darkened with age and smoke. "It's a pretty thing, isn't it?"

Maggie nodded, not wanting to interrupt.

"I was in here a few days ago, looking at what the workers had done, considering what might go well in here once it was all put back together. I was thinking about what I would put on the mantel, and I noticed something that didn't quite look right."

"Mrs. Ravenhurst," Doris began, worry in her eyes. "Should you—"

"It's all right, Doris," Mrs. Ravenhurst said. She turned back to Maggie and continued. "There was a little groove on the end. I bet you wouldn't notice it if the mantel was still over the fireplace."

Maggie squinted at the piece, trying her best to see something out of the ordinary, and then she pointed. "That leaf? It's almost like the others . . . but it looks like it might have a seam all the way around it."

Mrs. Ravenhurst nodded. "All my years in this house, and I never looked that closely at it. I suppose it's because it was never turned on end like that. Go ahead, push it."

Intrigued, Maggie pushed the leaf and it made a little

clicking sound. She looked up at Mrs. Ravenhurst when nothing else happened.

"Pull the end out," the older woman said.

Maggie gave it an uncertain tug, and still nothing happened. With the little carved buds and leaves poking into her palm, she pulled harder, then harder again, and a long, narrow drawer slid out of the end of the mantel.

Maggie blinked. "Oh."

Mrs. Ravenhurst nodded. "You can imagine how surprised I was. But it wasn't empty then." She turned to Doris. "Please go get it."

Doris glanced at Maggie and then reached into the pocket of her robe. "I thought, after what Hugh told me, you might want it." She pulled out a small, leather-bound book and put it into Mrs. Ravenhurst's waiting hand. "And this." She placed the gleaming emerald ring on top of it. "I didn't know what he'd done, ma'am, I swear. But I knew how much all this was upsetting you, and I told him how much I wished there was a way to get the ring for you. I never dreamed he'd try to do something about it himself."

"It's all right," Mrs. Ravenhurst assured her. "Don't worry. I don't blame Hugh." She turned to Maggie, holding up the ring. "And you don't have to worry either. I'll return this to the rightful owner. That girl's mother, I understand."

"Yes. But what in the world is in that book that was so upsetting?"

Mrs. Ravenhurst pressed her lips together, and what looked like pride and remorse and shame fought one another in her expression. "This," she said, "is the diary of Caroline Lacey Ravenhurst, written on the eve of her death. She . . . oh, I can't go through it again. It will seem trivial to you, especially after nearly three centuries, but I was raised to revere the name of

Ravenhurst, to take pride in its history and in the eminence of my ancestors. And to find this out now . . ."

She closed her eyes and shook her head.

"What does the diary say?" Maggie asked.

Doris took Mrs. Ravenhurst's arm. "Maybe we should go back into the parlor and sit down."

"Not yet," Mrs. Ravenhurst said, pulling free from her and then opening the little book, carefully turning the brittle pages until she found the one she wanted. "There. The worst of it is there."

She thrust the book into Maggie's hands and then gave her the flashlight she held. Maggie shone it on the open page, a page covered with the most beautiful copperplate script she had ever seen.

I have ever said (to those who made so bold as to ask) that I remember nothing of my kidnapping and escape, but that, alas, is a falsehood, a falsehood for which I pray our good Lord will forgive me. I had hoped by the time I reached such an age—I am well past my sixtieth year—that I would be able to unburden myself of this secret and, indeed, shout aloud the blessing I have received in what at first seemed like irrecoverable disaster.

I have long been taught to return blessing for cursing and good for evil. How difficult it was, you may well imagine, to speak kindly to those who stole me from my father's house in the hope that he would pay a rich ransom for my return. How difficult to hold fast to my trust that I was held in the hands of God Himself and that no true harm could befall me there.

The pirates, for so they were, were in the service of the

notorious Captain Solomon Zane, the very villain who had terrorized our coast since before my birth. They were rough men, unlearned, unwashed, and foul of speech, but such was their duty to their captain (or their fear of him) that they would not disobey his command that I should be gently treated until the time my ransom was paid.

However, there was one among them, a young man, tall and lithe, merry of eye and quick of wit, not at all akin to the others in Zane's service. I soon found that he was in truth the son of that same pirate, and his name was Remembrance Zane. Though he was the son of a notorious outlaw, he had the manners and bearing of a gentleman, for he had been raised up by his mother's people until her death, and had been tutored in all that might profit a gentleman in business and society. But when he was seventeen years of age, his father carried him away to the South Seas with his crew and taught him his vile trade.

But he had been taught the fear of God from his mother's knee and from all her people, and he could never bring himself to shed another man's blood or dishonor a woman or harm the truly defenseless. He told me I need not worry for my safety while I was their prisoner, and somehow I believed him. He had convinced his father that the name of Solomon Zane was enough to terrorize anyone, and so it had proved. In fact, the formidable captain did not leave his cabin as ever I saw. Each morning the first mate, a Razor Drummond, and the captain's son would go into the captain's cabin and reemerge with his orders for the day.

For the ten days I was a prisoner, hidden in a cove north

of Somerset Harbor, we talked often. He admitted that he longed to leave that life, to earn his way with honest labor, to begin again without the name of Zane and the dread of the law overshadowing him. And then, much to my surprise, he revealed to me the secret he and the first mate had kept hidden for almost half a year: The monster Solomon Zane had died of a wasting fever on an unknown island of the Pacific Ocean, and his crew had carried on, frightening their victims into submission merely by the use of his name.

I could not help pitying him any more than I could help wishing the circumstances of our meeting had been different. As it was, over the time of my captivity I convinced him that he could indeed start again, that our Lord made the free gift of new life to all who would come to Him, and that this new life could be temporal as well as spiritual. In the end, he gathered up some provisions, what he could of the gold and jewels his father had hoarded over his long career, and a ring that his father had been fond of wearing. That night, while he alone had the watch, we slipped over the side and swam ashore.

We made our way down the coast to Somerset Harbor unseen and parted where the forest meets the beach, and it was there that the pirate Solomon Zane vanished from the seas. Without Remembrance to talk sense into him, Drummond apparently decided to try piracy under his own name. As I had sworn, I told no one the story or what had befallen me during that time. It was more than a year later that my father told me he had met a gentleman named Evander Ravenhurst. Of course I could not tell Father that young Mr. Ravenhurst and I had met before.

By now Maggie was smiling. *Of course!* It came back to her as clearly as if the picture of Evander Ravenhurst's gravestone were right in front of her. *A Memorie departed.* A memory. A remembrance. Remembrance Zane.

"He came back and married her, didn't he? He made a whole new life for himself and made up for the wrongs his father had done."

"How could she?" Mrs. Ravenhurst's face was a mixture of horror and shame. "How could she lower herself to such a match? How could she taint the blood of her children and their children and all those after them with the blood of a thief and a cold-blooded murderer? After her own family line had been quite above reproach?"

"Maybe," Maggie said gently, "because she loved him."

"You don't understand," Mrs. Ravenhurst said. "Oh, how could I expect anyone to understand? I've lived all my life as a Ravenhurst. I—I drove away my . . ." She squeezed her eyes shut. "I drove away people that I love because I made it impossible for them to live up to my standards."

"Your granddaughters?"

"My granddaughters," Mrs. Ravenhurst said, her eyes still closed. "And the man I loved."

Maggie didn't dare press her for the story. "I'm so sorry," she murmured instead.

"He wasn't good enough, my mother said, and even though the name he had wasn't much of a name, he absolutely refused to change it to Ravenhurst. I've regretted losing him every day since I sent him away." She blotted her face with her handkerchief once more and then lifted her head. "But I had the impeccable Ravenhurst name, you see, and that was enough."

Until now. Oh, the poor woman.

"Mrs. Ravenhurst—" Maggie broke off, turning the light on the window opening she had come through. "Who's there?"

A pair of big dark eyes peered around the window frame. "It's me. Abby."

"Abby." Maggie sighed in relief. "It's all right. Come in."

Abby stepped over the sill and scurried into the room, looking uncertainly at Mrs. Ravenhurst. "I—I didn't mean to eavesdrop, but I wanted to make sure you were all right. And then I heard what you were talking about, and it sounded interesting. Like a real romance."

"Interesting." Mrs. Ravenhurst sniffed. "Interesting is all well and good, but you have no idea what it's like finding out something like this about your family."

Abby shrugged. "I guess it *is* my family, but maybe you didn't know that. I only found it out a little while ago."

"What do you mean, girl?"

"Don't you know? We're, um, what was it, Maggie?"

Maggie bit her lip, trying not to giggle at the look on Mrs. Ravenhurst's face. "Third cousins, twice removed. Mrs. Ravenhurst's great-grandfather was the brother of your father's great-great-grandmother."

Mrs. Ravenhurst looked the girl over as if seeing her for the first time, but she didn't say anything.

"Hey, what are you doing up here anyway?" Maggie asked suddenly. "You weren't supposed to get out of the car."

"I know," Abby said. "But then Mr. Peters came and got in his car and drove off, so I thought I'd better come up and see if you were okay."

"Abby! You were supposed to call 911 if he came down before I did."

"I know." Abby winced a little. "But he didn't see your car. And one of my friends got in trouble for prank-calling 911.

I didn't want to call if I wasn't sure you needed help. And . . . um . . . you didn't."

Maggie shook her head, not sure how to respond to that. It may not have been the soundest feat of reasoning, but at least everything had turned out all right. "Abby, what you overheard is very important to Mrs. Ravenhurst, and you can't tell anybody about it, do you understand?"

"Sure. I won't say anything to anybody, but I don't understand why. I think it's a great story."

"It's an embarrassment to the whole family," Mrs. Ravenhurst said. "That's what it is."

Abby looked thoughtful. "I guess what I liked was that he got a chance to start over, no matter what kind of family he was born into or what kinds of mistakes he made on his own. He got a chance to be a better person and do good stuff for the rest of his life. Why shouldn't we be proud he's part of our family?"

Mrs. Ravenhurst looked at her with a mixture of impatience and gentleness. "He was a thief and a murderer, child."

"Not a murderer," Abby insisted. "She said in that book that he didn't kill anybody."

"But he was a pirate. He stole things from people. It's an absolute scandal."

Abby lifted her chin and looked the older woman in the eye. "I used to steal things."

Maggie glanced at Mrs. Ravenhurst.

"I stole that ring," Abby said, pointing, "from my own mother."

Mrs. Ravenhurst's thin lips were pressed together, and her expression was very cool.

"But I knew it was wrong." There was an appealing earnestness in Abby's heart-shaped face. "I hated that I did it. I didn't want to be that way. I'm doing my best to make up for it. Is that no good? Shouldn't I even try?"

"Well, certainly," Mrs. Ravenhurst fumbled. "It's best to stop doing wrong and to make restitution. Naturally, it is."

"But it doesn't really matter if I do or don't, right?" Abby pressed. "Because I'm still a thief and won't ever be any good."

"I..." Mrs. Ravenhurst glanced at Maggie, her brow furrowed, and then turned again to Abby. "No, of—of course not. Of course you should be able to make amends and start again."

"Wouldn't you want to start over if you could?" Abby asked her, and then she turned faintly pink. "Not that you have stuff you need to be sorry for, but if you did?"

Mrs. Ravenhurst pressed her lips together once more, but even in the dim light, Maggie was sure they trembled a bit. "If I thought I could ever be forgiven for . . ." She pressed her mouth with her already damp handkerchief. "Well, for whatever I might have done."

"But that's what makes the pirate's son's story so cool," Abby said. "He *was* forgiven. At least that girl must have forgiven him for being part of her kidnapping, since she married him and all. And he did start over. He made his life better and helped people instead of hurting them. And he started a good family. I think that's something to be proud of."

Mrs. Ravenhurst studied Abby's young face. "I hadn't quite thought of it that way."

"I guess nobody would have any friends if people couldn't ask forgiveness and start over."

"No," Mrs. Ravenhurst said, and her voice was very soft. "Not many anyway."

Maggie didn't say a word. Her heart was full of the warmth and tenderness unfolding before her.

A moment later Mrs. Ravenhurst lifted her chin and nodded serenely at her housekeeper. "I think we all need a hot cup of tea, if it's not too much trouble, Doris. I think I'd like to get to know my cousin here a little better." She put her arm through the girl's, patting her hand as they began to walk back toward the habitable part of the house with Doris scurrying ahead of them. "I'd like to keep the ring, if it's all right. It'll be my reminder that even an old dog can learn a new trick. In exchange, we'll see that you and your mother have all the things you need. Do you think that's a fair trade?"

Abby beamed at her. "That would be great, um, Mrs.—"

"There has to be something less stuffy you could call me besides Mrs. Ravenhurst."

"Uh, I don't . . ."

"I know that, in some tenuous way, you and I are cousins, but how would it be if you called me Aunt Willa? It's been some while since I had someone to spoil a bit, but I don't think I've entirely forgotten how."

Maggie smiled as she watched them walk away. There was nothing more to add.

· · · · · · · · · · · · · · · · ·

"I don't believe it." June shook her head in amazement. "Mrs. Ravenhurst? Really?"

"Really," Maggie said, still hardly able to believe it herself. "She's letting me use the diary to write the story for the historical society. And she's paying to have professional photos taken of the ring, the portraits of Evander and Caroline Ravenhurst, and their gravestones to use on the site. It'll make a wonderful article."

June laughed. "But 'Aunt Willa'? I don't think I can picture that."

"I think it's a big step for her. But I believe she's also tired of being the lonely old rich lady." Maggie couldn't help smiling. "And I wouldn't be surprised if she's working to patch things up with her granddaughters too."

"And what about dear Mr. Peters? He's not going to be

very happy about missing out on that best seller he's been dreaming of."

"We talked about him," Maggie admitted. "And that reminds me, I need to give him back his replica of the ring. Anyway, Mrs. Ravenhurst looked at one of the articles he wrote for his blog. I think she might let him write his story after all, if he'll agree to let her approve the content."

"Do you think he will?"

"He might not end up with the sensational and lurid book he had envisioned," Maggie said, "but it might turn out to be something of historical interest and a wonderful love story on top of that. I don't think he'll make the *New York Times* top ten, but it ought to be a hit in Somerset Harbor if nowhere else. And honestly, that's all it really should be."

JUNE'S TIPS FOR BETTER ANTIQUES HUNTING

1. Come Prepared

If you're looking for something specific for a certain spot in your home, bring a list of room or space measurements and an easy-to-carry tape measure. And be sure to measure your doorways too. You don't want to fall in love with a piece, cart it back home, and then find it doesn't fit in the room you wanted, or worse yet, you can't even fit it through your front door.

2. Cash is King

Determine how much money you're willing to spend and withdraw cash to bring with you. You can often negotiate a better price if you're willing to give the dealer cash on the spot.

3. Return at the End of the Day

If you're at an antiques fair and you haven't been able to haggle down the dealer to a certain price on a piece, return later in the day. The dealer may be willing to accept the offer then instead of having to pack up and cart the piece home again.

To discover all that country decorating has to offer and see the creative home decorating tips that inspire Maggie and her friends, check out the latest issue of *Country Sampler* at CountrySampler.com!